ALL THAT REMAINS

ALL THAT REMAINS

KELSEY GREYE

WESBROOK BAY
BOOKS
Vancouver, B.C.

Copyright Kelsey Greye 2014

Edited by Beverley Boissery
Interior Design by BDG Austin

Published by Wesbrook Bay Books, an imprint of The Wesbrook Bay Group
www.wesbrookbay.com

Cover Design by Graeme J. Friesen

All That Remains is Book I in the Lake Claire Series.
All that Remains is a work of fiction. The names, characters, places, and incidents portrayed in the story are the product of the author's imagination or have been used fictitiously. Any resemblance to actual persons, living or dead, businesses or companies, events, or locales, is entirely coincidental.

First edition

ISBN: 978-1-928112-09-9

Acknowledgments

I am blessed with so many people who enrich my journey as a writer. My grandparents, parents, brother, sister-in-law and extended family have encouraged me personally and sparked ideas for both conversations and characters. Thank you all for being exactly who you are. To the friends who cheer me on when I hit a wall, coax me out of frustration and, above all, are willing to both laugh and cry with me, you mean the world to me. My Thursday morning breakfast ladies: each of you provides me with much needed perspective, endless support and prayer and more laughter than I would have dreamt possible. Thank you. And my dear friend and fellow scholar, Amanda, God has given you the gifts of a brilliant mind and a soft heart. I've been so blessed by both.

Graeme, your artistic gifts and willingness to design my cover are appreciated more than I can say. I am honored to be your sister.

To Beverley Greenwood, who has taken a chance on this writer in process and has offered encouragement, correction, challenge and support, I am so grateful for your input and your advice.

And, always, my greatest thanks to my Lord Jesus Christ,

whose gentleness, strength and unfailing love won my heart as a child and have kept it close ever since. There is no greater love story than yours.

Dedication

To my wonderful grandparents, Dave and Martha. Thank you for my own "summers in Lake Claire" that included the gift of your love, the blessing of your time and memories that I will cherish always. God has overwhelmed me by truly blessing me with the heritage of those who fear His name (Ps. 61:5). I love you both so much.

I

———————

The wooden clapboard house stood stark and lonely against the dark blue-grey rain clouds. It was mid-afternoon, but darkness had already descended, and the skies grew more ominous by the minute. I stood calf-deep in grass that hadn't been cut for who knew how long, studying the house. White paint barely clung to the weathered boards, and the front porch sagged from neglect and the changing seasons. Fifteen years had passed, and yet it looked the same.

This house and I had history; one built on tragedy and mystery.

I wondered if the porch would hold my weight. I doubted it but was tempted to try anyway, just to be able to peek in the dusty windows. But the threatening skies convinced me that I should wait for another day to find out. I pulled my phone from the pocket of my brown corduroy jacket and snapped a picture, hoping I caught the heavy clouds and windblown grass along with the house. The sense of isolation they evoked matched my emotions. With one last look at the desolate place that had haunted my dreams since I was fourteen, I turned away.

The first drops of rain hit my face as I jogged toward my car. I stopped and tilted my face up while digging in my pocket for my keys. The clean, sweet-smelling air was almost potent enough to make me forget driving into town until I'd had my fill of wandering grassy fields pretending I was the heroine in an Austen or Bronte novel. The scent of rain never failed to transport me to worlds I'd only read and dreamt about.

If my grandparents weren't expecting me to join them for Sunday dinner, I probably would have indulged myself but there was no way I was going to bring the wrath of Jim and Rose Newton down on my head. Don't get me wrong, I love my grandparents. They were anchors for me during a time in my childhood when my family broke apart. Summer visits to Lake Claire held some of my favorite memories. As a shy teenager, I'd walked the town spinning dreams of what my future might hold with the house that stood barren and neglected behind me centering most of my thoughts. I longed to fill the ache of unbelonging I'd never been without, and there had always been an air of melancholy to the house behind me that whispered to my heart like a long-lost friend.

As I climbed into my little silver Toyota I smiled, feeling my heart bump in anticipation. I'd been planning for this day since I was seven years old. Lake Claire was the perfect place to make a life; I was certain then and certain now. Of course, at that point, the details of that life were quite a bit hazier. With a check over my shoulder and a peek at the side mirror, I shifted into drive and pulled out onto the highway, heading toward town. The clock on the dashboard showed me that I had seven minutes to make it to my grandparents' house before I'd be late for lunch. I could do that, I thought, and pressed down harder on the accelerator.

Within minutes, I pulled into the drive of a pleasant little bungalow that had the kind of worn look that told you the owners who cared for it were getting tired. I pulled a comb out of my purse and quickly ran it through my brown chin-length hair before swiping on shimmering lip gloss. I grabbed my purse, climbed out of my car, and headed through the gate and around to the back door of my grandparent's house.

"Hello!" I called, opening the door after a quick knock. "Grandma and Grandpa, are you here?"

"In the kitchen – come on in."

I slipped my shoes off and shrugged out of my jacket before walking down a short hall-way to arrive in the bright, cheery kitchen. My grandfather rose from the table and gave me a firm hug, the bristles on his cheeks scratching my chin. I was nearly six feet tall and towered over my five foot, four inch grandfather, always feeling like an awkward giant next to him.

"It's nice to see you again, Wynne. Your grandmother was beginning to worry that you had run into trouble somewhere. There are dangerous people on the roads these days, particularly for a woman traveling by herself."

I wondered what he would think if he knew I'd been out to the Jackson house. Better off not mentioning that little detail, I thought before responding aloud.

"Oh, no more so than for a man traveling by himself, I suppose. I don't think highways can tell the difference between the sexes."

As usually happened when I was tired, my sarcastic mental imp ran for freedom. Honesty, good, I reminded myself, smart remarks, counter-productive. I turned to the small, round woman stirring soup that was simmering fragrantly in a pot on the stove and wrapped an arm around her shoulders. Her soft, white hair smelled like flowers amid the savory odor of broth and chicken. "Hi, Grandma," I said, giving her a gentle squeeze and then releasing her. "Sorry if I'm a little late."

She glanced up and smiled absently. "Well, you're here now, aren't you? I think we'll just leave the soup simmering on the stove, but everything else can go on the table. Wynne, why don't you sit in between us? We want to hear all about your plans."

We settled ourselves and the table and, after pausing to give thanks, began to eat. "I assume," my grandfather asked, clearing his throat, "you're still intending to live over the store, Wynne? I don't know if that's a wise decision."

"The apartment is included in the mortgage I'm paying on the building. It doesn't make sense to pay rent somewhere else when I can stay there. Besides, it's a beautiful old place with hardwood floors and plenty of sunlight from the picture window. Two bedrooms are more than I need but I can use one as an office and save space in the store."

"But you'll be living alone, won't you? Even in a small town like Lake Claire, that may not be the safe. We worry about you, dear."

"I think God will keep me safe just as well there as anywhere else, don't you?" I finished my soup and pushed the bowl away from me, ready to change the subject. "Did I tell you I'm planning to have my grand opening on Wednesday? The sign is ready and will be installed Tuesday afternoon. I can hardly wait to see it!"

"What are you calling it again?" Grandma's bright blue eyes were curious.

"Wynne's Books. I thought about calling it It's About Tome but Mom convinced me that might just be confusing."

The blank looks both grandparents gave me confirmed that my mother's advice was sound. I opened my mouth to explain the name and then shut it again. It wasn't worth the effort. "Well, I should probably be on my way, Grandma, Grandpa," I said, pushing my chair back and rising. "I still need to unload everything from my car and unpack this afternoon. I want to rest up tomorrow after church and then organize the store on Monday and Tuesday. I'm going to attend Lake Claire Community instead of Bethel Baptist," the latter was the church they'd always attended, but I felt the former, pastored by old college friends of mine, would be a better fit for me, "but don't worry! You'll still see lots of me. It's not like I'm joining some cult."

I winced as soon as the words left my mouth. I couldn't have chosen a worse comparison if I'd tried.

"I'm sorry. I know how rough things were here in town when that bizarre group got a foothold, especially after the Jacksons disappeared." I tried to smooth the feathers I'd inadvertently ruffled. "Didn't they disband shortly after that, though? I haven't heard anything more than whispers about the Children of the Elements in the past fifteen years."

My grandfather hitched his thumbs through the loops of his suspenders and cleared his throat gruffly.

"They're all gone now. Nobody would do business with them after the Jackson family disappeared. The whole town knew that cult had something to do with it but the police could never prove it. We carried out our own kind of justice and made it clear that they weren't welcome here. They got the hint and moved on."

"Who owns the Jackson house now?" I tried not to let my voice convey how much I wished it was me. That would only give my grandparents one more thing to worry over. "The family never did turn up, did they?"

"No, they didn't," answered my grandmother. "About seven years after they disappeared, there was talk that they could be declared dead and their property sold off. Kevin Ferris hovered around like a vulture trying to push the issue until the lawyers found out that the property actually belongs to Mr. Jackson's brother. He lives somewhere out west, doesn't seem to want to sell and barely keeps the house up, but he pays the taxes. You know what those Ferris boys are like, Wynne–always wanting what isn't theirs. They've been that way for generations."

I had to smile at my grandmother's description of the Ferris family. I'd played with Kevin when we were kids, and he'd always tried to steal my toys. She was absolutely right.

"When I drove past, it still looked abandoned. Nobody's live there since the Jacksons disappeared?"

"Nobody lives there and nobody has for the past fifteen years, but Mr. Jackson's brother won't sell. Linda Robins–you know that real estate lady with the big teeth and tight suits?" I smirked at Grandma's description, coughing to cover a giggle. "Well," Grandma sailed on, "she said she got in touch with him to ask him why. He still believes that his sister and her family might come back some day. It's sad, but that's the truth of the matter."

"That is sad." I took another step toward the back stairs. "Well, thanks again for lunch, Grandma and Grandpa. I'm sure I'll see quite a bit of you now that I'm living here."

"We'd love to have you any time you're not too busy. I hope you don't forget us once you have the store up and running."

"I could never forget you guys," I enfolded my grandmother in a firm hug before doing the same to my grandfather.

"We love you, sweetie."

"I love you, too." I grabbed my jacket and purse, slipping on my shoes. "See you soon!" I called over my shoulder as I breathed in the crisp spring air, making my way through the gate to my car in the driveway. I looked up as I pulled out of the drive and waved at my grandparents who stood silhouetted in the front window. With a final smile and wave, I headed on my way. I'd forget about the house and my dreams. The store, my new life, was what mattered now.

2

The building that would soon house both me and my business stood on Main Street. The brick was old; its faded red made more noticeable by bright white imitation marble trim. Up until a month ago, it had been Mr. Patterson's Old-Fashioned General Store. When I was a kid, I'd stop by on hot summer days for a milkshake and a bag full of penny candies. Every time I walked through the door, with its cheery bell announcing my arrival, my spirits lifted. Mr. Patterson himself always told me what a pretty girl I was and asked what I was up to. There was always a book nearby, face down by the cash register while he waited on customers and, as I was seldom without one myself, we ended up comparing what we were reading. To my surprise, I actually had a lot to say on the subject and a genuine friendship was born.

We kept in touch over the years through cards and letters in which he wrote all the town news. When I came back to Lake Claire after a difficult post-college job, Mr. Patterson took one look at me, sat me down at the high wooden counter on a tall, sturdy stool, and turned without a word to make me a chocolate milkshake. He set it in front of me, waiting until I took a sip. Then he looked me in the eye and told me that if I didn't make a change, I was going to burn out completely and become more miserable than I clearly already was.

"If you hang on to the bitterness that you have inside you, it's going to eat you alive, Wynne," he told me flatly. "You've got to forgive whoever you're holding a grudge against, get out of that job you hate, and let it go."

I cried. All the things I'd been keeping bottled up spilled out, and I sobbed into my milkshake. When I finally calmed down, the drink was melted and my face was swollen and blotchy from tears. I'd never been a pretty crier. Mr. Patterson just took away my melted shake, set a fresh one in front of me, handed me his handkerchief and asked me what I was going to do now.

"Get therapy," I'd responded, only half in jest. "Get a life."

"That sounds like a good idea, Wynne," he said, eyes serious. "I have a few ideas on that, if you'll hear me out."

I nodded my agreement, too exhausted from my breakdown to speak.

"Here's what I think. You're not cut out to work with peoples' problems day in and day out in the way you have been, but," he held up a finger, "you're great at dealing with the public. You just invest too much sometimes, and the job you had took advantage of that. Didn't give you any breathing room," he muttered, shaking his head.

"You can say that again."

"Well, that's the past. No sense in dwelling on it. You used to talk about moving to Lake Claire all the time. Is that still your dream?"

"I don't know," I spoke slowly, my voice hoarse from my fit of weeping. "I love this town and would move here in a heartbeat if I thought I could make a living, but I just don't see how I could."

"If you want to live here, I think I have a way to make it happen."

"How? I mean, what could I do?"

"Turn your love of books into a career. The town doesn't have a bookstore, and I know people want one. Customers are always griping about the lack of selection."

"Do you really think so, Mr. Patterson?" I felt hope rising inside me, but it sank as a thought occurred. "But that would eat into your profits. I couldn't do that!"

"Well, here's the second part of my plan. I'm old, Wynne," he said and laughed when I automatically shook my head to deny it, "I am. I turned seventy this year, and it's time I retired. I don't want to sell this place to just anyone, but for you...well, you could give it what it needs. The town doesn't need a general store anymore. Most people shop out at the big box store near the highway. The space would be great for a bookstore, and, if you buy the building from me, you can have the apartment upstairs to live in."

"But that's where you live." I protested. "Where will you go?"

"I have some ideas already," he smiled enigmatically. "Don't worry. I won't be far away, but my time as a storeowner is just about done. I'm not up to the work anymore and I want to sell to someone I trust. What do you think?"

I took a deep breath, my mind whirling. "I think I'm going to need to pray about this, but...oh, Mr. Patterson, it feels right."

"Take the time you need, and we'll talk again. I'm not selling to anyone else, and I've got a couple of years left in me to work. I'm just planning for the future, and I think it's a good fit for you too."

"I think you're right. I'll let you know as soon as I decide."

He patted my hand, his wrinkled face creasing as he smiled. "You're a good girl, Wynne. You'll be fine."

That conversation had taken place two years ago and, finally, my dream was real. When I parked my little car around the back of the store, it felt strange. That spot that had always belonged to Mr. Patterson's olive green station wagon, but from here on out it was mine. It took twelve trips from my car to the apartment to get everything unloaded. By the time I carried the last suitcase inside, sweat was dripping off my forehead and into my eyes, blurring my vision. and I sent up a prayer of gratitude that the apartment was fully furnished. I shut the door and stood with my hands on my hips, surveying my domain.

Nudging boxes aside, I made a narrow path from the door into the center of the living area. I looked over the neat markings on each box and opened the first one I found labelled "bedroom". By four o' clock, all I had left were two empty suitcases and some flattened boxes stored in the closet of the second bedroom. I grabbed my jacket from where I'd draped it over the back of a chair and pulled my keys from the pocket. I picked up my purse and headed for the door, locking it behind me. Groceries for the coming week and take-out for supper so I could relax on the couch while watching a movie in my new living room sounded like the perfect way to end a long day.

I didn't see anyone I recognized in either the grocery store, or as I walked down the street to pick up supper from Trudy's Family Restaurant, and I was glad. I was ready for small town life, I thought, but one final evening of anonymity was nice. Soon enough I wouldn't be able to leave my apartment or the store without running into customers and friends. The prospect was more than a little daunting, especially for a bookworm like me. I pushed open the door to Trudy's and breathed in the scent of home-cooked meals, vinyl booths and years gone by.

A teenage girl hurried to the kitchen to grab my take-out order. For less than an appetizer would cost in the city, I headed out the door with a large Styrofoam container of rosemary chicken with roasted potatoes. I sipped the large diet Coke I'd ordered with my meal as I walked back to my new home, feeling more contented than I had for years. As I climbed the stairs and unlocked the door, my thoughts returned to the Jackson house. Its air of loneliness drew me to it, even when it was inhabited by the Jackson family. Now that they were gone, the lonely quality had morphed into something darker that was nearly as tantalizing.

It was a house with secrets.

That summer fifteen years ago still haunted me. I could still see Amy Jackson's dark eyes watching me as I awkwardly rode my grandfather's bike past the wooded area about two miles from the Jackson house where the Children of the Elements met to worship their gods and goddesses. No one outside the group knew much about what went on during their ceremonies. To tell the truth, no one really wanted to know. All I knew then was that there was something dark and dangerous in the eyes of the leaders, and something entirely different in the followers. The look I saw in Amy Jackson's eyes that humid August day was fear–stark, bone-deep terror.

I'd wanted to help, but there was nothing I could think of to do. There was nothing obviously wrong happening. Still, so unsettled by the heaviness I felt, I rode back to town and the safety of my grandparents' house for all I was worth. When I finally worked up the nerve to ride out to the Jackson house the next morning to see if Amy wanted to go to the general store with me, it was too late.

Amy was gone, along with her parents and older brother. I'd looked through the windows on the main floor after knocking several times. It was as though they simply disappeared, leaving the table set for dinner and car in the dirt driveway.

I peddled into town and told Mr. Patterson the whole story. He closed the store, put my bicycle in the back of his station wagon, drove out to the Jackson house, and checked the hood of the car for warmth to see if it had been driven recently.

Looking back, our attempts at solving the mystery were naïve, but at least they were sincere. We thought about breaking in to be sure the family was not somehow incapacitated. Then a police car drove up. A passing motorist had called in suspicious activity around the Jackson place, having seen us as they drove by.

I told the officer that I thought something bad had happened to the Jackson family. When he asked why I thought that, I told him it was just a feeling I had because Amy Jackson had looked frightened the last time I saw her. He clearly thought the intuition of an insecure, overweight fourteen year old girl with thick glasses was hardly worth his time. He sent me home with Mr. Patterson after extracting a promise that I wouldn't come back out to the Jackson place without an invitation from the family themselves.

I'd watched and listened for news of the Jacksons for the rest of the summer, and for years after, but there was nothing. Amy was gone. They were all gone.

3

The house was a hulking black shadow in the moonlight; no lights within to soften its stark outline. A shiver ran down my spine as I stepped through the dew-wet grass and moved closer to the sagging porch. The inner door was wide open, an unspoken invitation into the darkness inside. I gripped the slim flashlight I'd tucked into the pocket of my hooded sweatshirt and pulled it out, flicking the switch to turn it on. A thin circle of light illuminated the entrance: the hall table and the little pottery bowl with keys still sitting in it. I swung the light to the left and took a step forward, stumbling as my foot landed on a rotten board and plunged through it. I fell to my left, landing face first on the porch. My hands slid across the rough wood, the skin of my palms shredding as I tried to break my fall. My flashlight landed in front of me, rolling until it was shining right in my eyes. I raised an arm to shield myself from the glare and grabbed it, wincing as my injured hand closed around the cool metal cylinder.

I pushed myself up onto my knees and then my feet, still bent over as

I used my hands to gain leverage. The light shone through the cracks in the porch and my stomach clenched as it played over the dirt beneath. A gleam caught my eye. As I dropped to my knees and leaned closer, and a scream rose in my throat as my mind tried to take in what I saw. There in the weak beam of my flashlight, reaching up as though I could grasp it and pull her to life was a skeletal hand, still wearing the thin, glimmering gold wedding band that had caught my eye.

I woke with a start, pushing myself to a sitting position before I was even aware of what I was doing. I reached over and turned on the bedside lamp, taking deep breaths to calm my frantically beating heart. I'd had versions of the same horrible dream ever since Amy Jackson and her family went missing. At first, it had come every night. As the years passed it happened less frequently, with months of peaceful sleep between emergences. It occurred most often during the summer months, the time of year when the family actually disappeared. Obviously being back in Lake Claire brought the memories closer to the surface.

I ran a hand through my hair and rubbed my neck, trying to dispel the residual tension. I swung my legs over the side of my bed and stood, stretching my arms over my head. It was just past 6am, nearly time to rise anyway. I pulled the drapes open and breathed in the cool morning air drifting through the open window and soothing my heated forehead. I moved to the dresser and quickly swapped my cotton pyjamas for a pair of stretchy yoga pants, a tank top and zip-up hooded sweatshirt.

Leaving my pyjamas on the rumpled bed, I walked through the apartment to the entrance, grabbing my phone from the kitchen table, and hit the street at a fast walk. I loved walking, especially in the early morning. It was the best time of day for me to pray and think, and the exercise helped lift my spirits. Turning my face to the east, I set off down Main Street pretending to myself that I wasn't going to end up walking a loop that would lead me directly past to Jackson house.

There is a moment, right after the sun rises but before the dew evaporates, when the world seems fresh and unflawed. It feels peaceful and exciting at the same time. It always reminds me that God's mercies are new every morning which, for a guilt-ridden perfectionist like me, is golden. Considering the amount of times God reiterates that theme in the Bible, I have a sneaking suspicion that he knows his creation well. That he knows me completely and doesn't hold my sins, my flaws and my failures against me is a kind of love that I still can't wrap my head around. I lengthened my stride while thinking about this, swinging my arms easily in rhythm to the music flowing through my earbuds.

I came to the edge of town and kept moving steadily down the highway, sticking to the shoulder. I fiddled with my phone again, scrolling through music until I found what I was looking for. As the old, abandoned farmhouse came into sight, a wordless Celtic lament filled my ears. In the early morning light, the house was not the fearsome, haunted thing it was in my dreams. It was simply worn out and sadly neglected. I stopped for a minute and took it in, wishing I had the right to fix it up and that I had family and children to fill it with laughter and life.

Recognizing that I was slipping in daydreams when I needed to be heading home, I turned around and started back toward my apartment. I didn't bother to tell myself I should find a new route for my walk tomorrow. I wouldn't have listened anyway–and perhaps it was time to own the kinship I felt with this place instead of hiding it. With a final glance over my shoulder at the house silhouetted in the growing light of day, I lengthened my stride, flicked my phone back to more energetic music and turned my mind to the day ahead. Church started at ten so I had plenty of time to shower and put myself together. Before any of that, however, I needed to say hello to my coffee maker and start it percolating so that blessed first cup of coffee would be waiting for me once I was ready for the day.

I quickened my pace as the apartment came into view. I could practically smell the enticing scent of brewing caffeine. I jogged up the stairs and unlocked the door, pulling it shut behind me and kicking off my shoes. I stretched, groaning at the pull in my shoulders and back. The walk had loosened my muscles up after yesterday's drive but I could still definitely feel the hours spent sitting in my car. I yanked off my hat and ran a hand through my messy, sweaty hair. I walked into the kitchen, hit the start button on the coffee maker and then headed to the shower.

Thirty minutes later, I walked out of my bedroom wearing a white cotton eyelet dress with thin straps and a short blue shrug. The dress fell to my knees in a graceful sweep from a waist that tied in the back with a sash. It was my favourite one and that was saying something because I had a weakness for pretty things. When I was a little girl, I had white eyelet curtains framing the window in my bedroom. The fabric was a reminder of the innocence and sweetness that had been all too brief parts of my childhood. The screaming matches and many days when Dad just didn't come home at all while Mom sobbed into her pillow made my home more of a war zone than a sanctuary. They eventually worked things out, and we were close now, but those early years left a mark on us all.

Rolling my shoulders, I pushed the memories aside and reached into the cupboard for a mug. I had a motley assortment of mugs with no two matching in the bunch. The one I pulled out this morning was wide and round with a frowning face on it. It always made me smile. For some reason, I didn't find the companion mug with a smiley face nearly as charming.

I poured myself a cup of steaming hot coffee and set it aside to cool a bit while I got my breakfast ready, slipping bread into the toaster, and then pulled an unopened jar of strawberry jam from the cupboard next to the mugs. I grabbed an apple out of the fridge and quickly sliced it into a small bowl and then slathered a thin layer of jam onto the toast that popped up just as I finished doctoring my coffee with honey.

I brought everything over to the table and sat down, taking a book from the pile of novels already stacked on the table. I usually had one of every genre out, since I never knew what mood I'd be in. This morning's pick was an Agatha Christie murder mystery. It was an old, familiar friend and I lost myself in the pages while I ate.

I glanced at my watch and realized that I needed to get going if I wanted to be on time for church. I downed the last of my coffee, rinsed my dishes and stuck a bookmark in the book I'd placed face down on the table. I took a quick look in the mirror to make sure I didn't have food on my face or dress and then grabbed my keys and purse, slipping my feet into a pair of flats. I locked the door behind me and hurried down the stairs, hitting the street at a swift walk. A smile flitted across my face as I turned toward the church. It was time to become a member of the community.

I could hardly wait.

4

Lake Claire Community Church was a simple wooden building on the corner of 3rd and Elm. The white clapboard gleamed in the mid-morning sunlight and the high tower echoed with the ringing bells. It had been an Anglican church in my youth, but the congregation had dwindled so badly that the diocese had agreed to sell the building to Lake Claire Community Church. Josh and Lise Taylor, former classmates of mines, had been the pastors there for the past seven years. I had become good friends with both of them during our college years. Whenever we saw each other, rare as that was, we fell back into our friendship easily. I could hardly wait to see how it would deepen now that we lived in the same town.

The solid wooden door was propped open, the soft breeze from outside following me into the foyer. It wasn't large, but it was open and airy with the ceiling fans twirling lazily overhead. I could see the sanctuary over to my right and the sight of sun-washed, pale wooden pews touched with a hint of the colour from the stained glass windows settled my soul and calmed the nerves that arose at the prospect of meeting new people.

"Wynne! I'm so glad you made it!" I grinned as Lisa hurried toward me, faster than I would have thought possible with a baby on her hip and a toddler in tow. "How was your drive? Are you all settled in at the apartment?"

"It was good and yes, I am." I gave her a hug. "It's so good to see you again, Lisa. Now, who are these little ones and how long have they belonged to you?"

She laughed and laid a hand on the head of the little blond-haired boy clinging to her leg and studying me with a serious expression on his small face.

"This is Oliver, and he's a little adult at two and a half. His sister, Julia, is the growth currently attached to my hip and she's almost one."

I smiled at Oliver and wiggled my fingers in greeting before letting Julia grab my index finger as I reached out to stroke her soft, plump cheek.

"You had to know that naming him after a Dickens character was going to make him a miniature adult–especially that particular Dickens character."

"I know, but at least we didn't name him Fagin," she chuckled.

"Or the Artful Dodger," I replied, crouching down and extending a hand to Oliver. He examined it for a moment before stretching out his tiny one to shake and my heart melted. "I think I'm a goner, Lisa," I murmured to my friend. "He's going to be a heartbreaker when he grows up. You and Josh make adorable kids."

She smiled back, the light reaching all the way to her eyes. Lisa wasn't pretty in a traditional sense. She was average height and weight with hair that is a nondescript brown when she didn't have it dyed – which is never. Since I'd known her, she'd been a redhead, blonde, brunette, and tried a shade of magenta I'd never seen on anyone's head before or since. Her hair was currently a pretty auburn that flattered her fair complexion. Her eyes are big, green and always alight with emotion of some sort. We'd made great roommates because I was hesitant to allow people in, and she was reticent with nothing. I'd never met a more giving person and probably never would.

"Come on, Wynne; you're sitting with us, right? Oliver, we're going to sit down now."

Without waiting for an answer, she tugged me toward the sanctuary. The last vestiges of tension from my restless night evaporated. I slid into the pew near the front of the sanctuary, moving toward the middle so Lisa could slide in behind me with the kids. I looked around curiously, wondering who, if anyone, I would see when I opened my store and what kinds of relationships would develop. Maybe I'd finally thrill my grandparents by meeting a kind, godly man I could make a life with. Just as that thought formed, my gaze landed on a tall, dark-haired man walking down the side aisle toward a pew near the middle of the sanctuary. His strong features were marked with gentleness as he sat down next to an elderly woman and asked her something I couldn't hear. I felt a flush creep up to my neck, and I quickly averted my eyes, hoping Lisa hadn't noticed my attention wandering.

We'd just sat down when the music began, and the worship and sermon seemed to fly by. Josh was a gifted preacher and his message on trusting God to direct our paths hit me right where it hurt. My head spun as Lisa introduced me to every person within a one mile radius. I was sure that I wouldn't remember most of their names but it was a good way to at least start getting to know my new neighbours. Once Josh had locked up the church and Lisa had strapped Oliver and Julia into their strollers, the five of us walked the short distance to Trudy's.

"Miss Wynne, what are you going to have?" asked Oliver. "I want pancakes. Do you like pancakes?"

"Sometimes," I replied gravely, hiding a smile at his earnest expression, "but today I think I feel like eating some vegetables. Do you like vegetables?"

A waitress with puffy white hair and sharp green eyes made her way over to our table and took an order pad out of the pocket of her apron just as Oliver made a face over the propsect of vegetables for lunch.

"Hello there, Josh, Lisa," she said, giving me a curious look. "What can I get you today?"

"The usual for us, Dot," replied Josh, "and Oliver will have the pancakes. That's what you want, Oliver?"

The little boy nodded and nudged his menu toward Dot.

"He can share with Julia," Lisa murmured, so that Oliver wouldn't hear. "This is Wynne Forrester, my college roommate. She's opening a bookstore in Mr. Patterson's old general store. Wynne, this is Dot Hennessy. She knows everything there is to know about this town and everybody in it."

"It's a pleasure to meet you," I said, smiling at the woman who was visibly sizing me up. I guessed that she was memorizing what I looked like so she could spread the news about my arrival later. She hadn't worked at the restaurant during my youth, but she certainly fit with my stereotypical image of the small town waitress who knew all the latest gossip. "I'll have tomato soup and a grilled cheese sandwich with a tossed salad to start."

The woman nodded, writing quickly, and then turned on the heels of her orthopaedic shoes and headed toward the kitchen. I wondered if Dot Hennessy had known the Jacksons and if she knew anything about the Children of the Elements. If Lisa was right, she was likely the best source of information I could find. I wanted to ask her about both but I wasn't sure how to bring it up without sounding like a busybody. Besides that, I needed to watch for a while and figure out if my questioning would get back to my grandparents. If that was going to be the case, I'd have to prepare myself for the backlash.

After lunch, I walked back to my apartment and curled up for the afternoon with The Blue Castle, one of my favourite books. I thought of the stacks of boxes waiting to be unpacked downstairs in the store but I'd made a promise to myself that I would take one day a week as a day to rest, at least. The nightmare from last night kept flashing through my mind despite my efforts to vanquish it, and I felt a growing sense of unease. By eight thirty, I was tired and ready to go to bed. I thumped my pillow with my fist and then bunched it into the crook of my neck. *Lord, please watch over me as I sleep and protect me from dreams of darkness, replacing them with your light.* As I closed my eyes in the dark, I said a final prayer–for Amy Jackson's safety, wherever she was. I just hoped it wasn't buried underneath the front porch of her old house.

5

Monday and Tuesday flew by in a blur. I unpacked boxes, organized bookshelves and created my first window display, which taxed my creativity to the limit. I was proud of the result, though.

The "Mysteries through History" theme allowed me to showcase books from a variety of genres. A glossy, richly-illustrated coffee table book of Egyptian history was propped open next to one on Stonehenge. I'd indulged my inner imp by prominently displaying a thick volume on cults and one on religions of the world, tucking them under a true crime novel about a missing woman. I wanted to remind the town that it had a history and mystery of its own, though I knew it might not be my smartest move. My problem, I muttered to the empty air, was that I couldn't seem to let the past go and I didn't want anyone else to either.

I picked up a leather bound copy of Jane Eyre and set it at

an angle to the true crime novel, bunching the dark red velvet I was using for a backdrop in what I hoped was an artistic manner between the two. I then added two Agatha Christie novels, an Anne Perry book and a beautifully bound copy of Jane Austen's Northanger Abbey. I knew my love of classic novels was showing, but the pleasing aesthetics of leather bound, gilt-edged volumes made them perfect for the display.

Wednesday dawned cloudy but calm. I thought it would be good advertising for me to be in public the morning I was opening the bookstore, and my grandparents were delighted to meet me for an early breakfast at Trudy's. I stepped into the restaurant five minutes before seven and smiled at Dot who greeted me with a combination of friendliness and appraisal. I figured she was still deciding if she liked me enough to spill all the gossip, or just the tidbits she shared with visitors.

"Dot, Josh and Lisa said that you know everything about Lake Claire. I wish I had that kind of memory! I was wondering if you could tell me who all these people are. The only ones I recognize are the sheriff and his deputies and that's only by virtue of their uniforms."

I was rewarded when she preened at the compliment and lowered the coffeepot to the table.

"Well," she said, pointing at the booth occupied by two men and woman in the brown uniforms indicative of rural law enforcement, "The older man with the shaved head is Sheriff Dan Black. He's been sheriff here for about ten years now. The younger man is his deputy, Luke Mason, and the young woman is our newest officer, Sophie Moore. Luke grew up in Lake Claire and his parents own Petals, the flower shop, just two doors down from here. Officer Moore came here six months ago from Chicago. She was a police officer in the city for seven years, I think."

"Seven years?" I was surprised. Sophie Moore barely looked old enough to have graduated from the police academy. I studied the slim, athletic brunette more closely, realizing from Dot's comment that she must be at least in her late twenties. Luke Mason, blonde and blue-eyed with the physique of someone devoted to the gym, looked to be in his early thirties. I didn't remember Luke Mason from my summer visits to Lake Claire but I'd spent most of my time with my grandparents and Mr. Patterson.

"She's older than she looks," Dot smiled over at Sophie, eyes softening with genuine affection. "And she's tougher than she looks too. Just last week, Trevor Powers was caught selling drugs at the middle school. He was a nasty, whiny boy and becoming a teenager hasn't changed that. Anyway, she was about to escort him to the police car when he took a swing at her. Quick as a flash, Sophie took out her baton thing while ducking and then cracked him with it. He went straight down, and she only hit him once! Of course, he was shouting about police brutality as soon as he woke up, but everybody there saw him try to punch her."

I grinned at the satisfaction in Dot's voice. I was going to like this woman a lot.

"I'll be sure to do my best to stay on her good side then," I said. I was about to ask another question when the door opened and my grandparents walked in. I waved them over to the table.

"Morning, Jim, Rose," Dot said, calmly filling their mugs, "what'll it be today? Do you want your usual?"

"Sounds good to me, Dot," Grandpa hitched a pant leg as he sat back. "What about you, Rose?"

"I think so," replied my grandmother without even glancing at the menu.

"And for you, Wynne?"

I felt an inordinate sense of triumph that Dot was now addressing me by name.

"I'll have the egg white omelette with cheese and green pepper, and brown toast."

The waitress nodded and briskly turned to walk to the kitchen without bothering to write the orders down. I smiled at my grandparents.

"How are both of you this morning? Did you sleep well?"

"Oh yes, as well as usual," Grandma's voice was shrill with excitement. "But what about you? Aren't you excited, Wynne? It's your opening day! We've told everyone we know about our wonderful granddaughter and her new store."

I bit back a laugh. While in some families my grandmother's statement would be an exaggeration; in mine, it most certainly was not. I had no doubt that both my grandparents had been regaling every one they met–friend, foe or stranger–with news of my store and probably my marital status. In just over an hour, I'd be opening my doors to the public for the first time. A wave of anxiety hit me, and I struggled to hide it, sipping my coffee methodically.

"Thanks, Grandma and Grandpa, I appreciate the free marketing. Are you going to come by once I open?"

"Of course we are. We'll be the first ones through the door when you open, and we want a picture of us standing with our beautiful granddaughter on such a special occasion. You look especially lovely today, Wynne."

I glanced down at my black knee-length shift dress and the

long, thin magenta cardigan cinched at the waist with a wide black leather belt. I had a long intricately-braided gold chain in my purse ready to put on after breakfast. "Thanks, Grandma. I'm glad you think so."

Dot arrived at the table with our food and we concentrated on our breakfasts for the next twenty minutes. I finished my last bite of toast just as my grandfather got up and walked over to the booth where the sheriff and his companions were just getting up. I tried not to blush when I heard him insist they come over to our table to meet his "single granddaughter who owned the new bookstore". I dabbed at my mouth with a napkin, hoping that I didn't have bits of green pepper in my teeth, scanning the room to see if anyone else had heard my grandfather's invitation. I flushed when my eyes caught the gaze of the dark-haired man I'd seen in church. His lips twitched and his deep green eyes held a gleam of amusement as he lifted his coffee cup in a friendly salute. Mortified, I stared down at my plate to compose myself before raising my gaze to watch my grandfather's return, with the police in tow.

"This is my granddaughter, Wynne Forrester. Wynne, this is Sheriff Dan Black, Deputy Luke Mason and Officer Sophie Moore. I've gotten to know them from my police ride-alongs through the Citizens on Patrol program. I go every Friday night."

His pride was evident in his voice and I grinned. Officer Moore caught my eye and winked, her wide brown eyes sparkling with fun.

"Jim's our most dedicated citizen helper," she said, giving him a friendly pat on the arm. "Just last week, he spotted a prowler by the Donaldson's house while they were on vacation and called it in. We got there in time to catch the guy trying to make his way out the back door with their 50" TV." She grinned, the freckles across her nose making her look like she was about sixteen. "It's hard to run away when you're carrying something that bulky."

I laughed. Glancing at my watch, I saw that it was time for me to go.

"It's a pleasure to meet you all," I said, pushing my chair back and standing up. "I'm sorry to eat and run, Grandma and Grandpa, but I need to get to the store. Maybe I'll see you later?" I let my questioning gaze encompass the police officers as well. No sense in wasting Grandpa's free marketing, I thought prosaically.

Oh, of course," Grandma nodded enthusiastically.

"We'll stop by too, Miss Forrester," said Sheriff Black in a gravelly voice that suggested smoking somewhere in his past. "It's good for us to show our support of new local businesses."

He smiled, but his light blue eyes stayed cool and flat. I gave him a polite smile and then turned the same smile to Deputy Mason. He stepped closer to me, offering his hand.

"It's a pleasure to meet you, too, Miss Forrester," Deputy Mason's grin seemed just a hair too friendly to me, "especially since we don't get many available young women who look as good as you here in Lake Claire."

I grimaced mentally as I tried to extricate my hand from his clinging grip. I could see my grandparents from the corner of my eye. Both were grinning like loons, and I swore that my grandmother was humming the wedding march under her breath. I sighed and stepped to the side, forcing the man to release my hand or be pulled with me. He let go reluctantly, and I didn't bother to hide the fact that I wiped my hand on my dress. Officer Moore started to snicker but changed it to a coughing fit when Deputy Mason glared at her.

"I look forward to seeing you all later," I said brightly. "I'm offering free coffee, tea and scones all day as a grand opening welcome."

I waved at Dot, tossed a ten dollar bill on the table to cover my breakfast and then hurried toward the door, breathing a sigh of relief as it swung shut behind me. I walked swiftly down the block, trying to shake off the feeling of unease the encounter with Luke Mason had left. I was over-sensitive around men, but past experience had taught me to trust my instincts. Deputy Mason had a lecherous air that made me feel like I needed to go home, shower off his too-thorough gaze, and only re-emerge if I was wearing a full-length shapeless potato sack. His blatant up and down scan had made me regret wearing my feminine sweater and pretty dress, and that near sense of shame quickly turned into anger.

I looked up at the old-fashioned wooden sign with a large open book and Wynne's Books etched into it swinging slightly in the breeze over the store doorway. I shoved my rising temper down determinedly and unlocked the door. Breathing in the comforting scent of leather, ink and paper, I walked behind the window display, plopped down on the floor to sit cross-legged and dropped my head into my hands. I had thirty minutes before I needed to unlock the door.

I let the air in my lungs out slowly and closed my eyes. "Lord, this day is yours and everything in it. Let me glorify you in all that I say and do—and, if you don't mind, I'd really like my shop to succeed. Give me wisdom to deal with customers and an open heart to your leading. Deputy Mason really creeped me out but I'm asking that you'll prompt me to pray for him and see him as someone who needs to know you. I'm asking that for all my customers; for new friends who know you and for the ability and opportunity to be a light to those who don't. Help me trust my future to You and You alone. Amen."

6

_____

The antique brass bell I'd hung at the entrance of the store tinkled merrily as the door swung open to admit my first customers. Mr. Patterson led the way with my grandmother and grandfather right behind him. Following them were Josh and Lisa with Oliver and Julia in tow.

"Welcome to Wynne's Books," I said, gesturing to the shelves behind me. "Please look around and help yourself to some coffee and a scone. If you have any questions, just ask."

"Oh, that sounds delicious! Josh, why don't you browse with Oliver while Julia and I visit with Mrs. Newton in the cafe? Is is all right, Mr. Newton," Lisa gave my grandfather a bright smile, "if we borrow your wife for a bit? Julia just loves her and I love having enough time to eat a scone and sip some coffee while someone else holds her."

"Of course, Mrs. Taylor," Grandpa's face softened at the sight of Julia's toothless grin. "My Rose does love little ones. We're hoping that sometime soon we'll be able to fuss over Wynne's babies – but we need to find her a nice young man first."

I started to roll my eyes, but caught myself. You can't, I thought firmly, treat customers poorly. Even if they're family, and even if what they say is embarrassing you. The knowing look Lisa gave me as she escorted my grandmother to the café told me she knew exactly what I was thinking and she was going to do her best to redirect the conversation–not because she felt sorry for me but because she knew I might say something I'd regret if things continued down that road. Now there's a true friend, I decided, turning back to watch the men wandering the aisles.

A combination of nerves and pride filled me as they examined the book displays and browsed. The worn, smooth mahogany counter from the general store was still in place, with its old-fashioned cash register. I'd even left the thick glass jars that used to be filled with penny candy there but had filled them with coloured stones that caught the light coming through the wide front window. Along the top of the wide counter, I'd placed trays with divine-smelling scones fresh from Sweet Delights Bakery and the coffee maker sputtered and gurgled as it brewed a pot of gourmet coffee.

I walked over to Mr. Patterson and gently slipped an arm around his stooped shoulders. He was wearing a brown cardigan over a white button-down shirt tucked into dark brown slacks. A bright red bow tie completed the look, and I recognized the combination as his best ensemble. I was touched that he considered my store opening worthy of it.

"It looks really nice in here, Little Wynne," he said, using the nickname he'd given me years ago. I'd never been all that little but the name was Mr. Patterson's way of making me feel special.

"I'm so glad you think so, Mr. Patterson. I was a bit worried that you wouldn't like the changes."

I gestured to the small café area just to the right of the window display, where Lisa and Julia were seated at a round table, my grandmother having rejoined her husband near a display. I wasn't going to offer much more than regular coffee, lattes and mochas, but I'd worked out a discount deal with Sweet Delights on baked goods and had high hopes that the added attraction of a cozy place to sit and read would inspire more purchases.

"No, I think you've done a great job with this place." He glanced around again, his gaze stopping on the milkshake machine still in place behind the counter. "You didn't get rid of that old thing?"

"How could I? It's an integral part of my childhood and besides, it'll be a good money maker on hot summer days when people don't want warm drinks."

"I noticed," he said, his eyes alight with amusement, that your window display has some interesting selections in it. No ulterior motives with any of any of those choices, ere there?"

I didn't even bother to pretend innocence. "Just wanted to do my part to remind this town that we have an unsolved mystery of our own that's as intriguing as any published story. You don't think it was too blatant, do you?"

"As if that would have stopped you, Little Wynne," he chuckled. "But no, odds are, nobody will even notice. We'll have to do some digging into the past on our own, once you're a bit more settled. I've got nothing but time on my hands right now."

Excitement stirred with the thought. Then Grandma, holding two large-print westerns in one hand and a cup of coffee in the other, walked up to us with Grandpa at her side. "We want to be your first customers, Wynne!" She bobbed toward the cash register with my grandfather in tow.

"I'd love that, Grandma. I'll be right there."

I gave Mr. Patterson's arm a pat and moved behind the counter to ring up the sale. The bell above the door jingled again as it opened and three middle-aged women I didn't recognize came in. I turned my attention back to working the register and saw that Lisa was now waiting in line with four books in her hands. I handed Grandma her books in a plastic bag and squeezed her hand in thanks as I gave her the receipt. I sent Grandpa a bright smile and waved as the two of them walked to the door and pushed it open, went through and then held it open for a group of teens to come in.

"Congratulations on the store, Wynne!" Lisa handed me her books and bounced on the balls of her feet in excitement. "It's beautiful and I just know I'm not going to be able to resist coming here far more often than I can really afford."

"Thanks, Lisa – and you know that you're welcome anytime, whether you buy anything of not. You're good for my ego."

"I hope that's not all I'm good for!" She went to join her husband, who was standing next to Julia's stroller with Oliver. "Thanks for the books and good luck today!"

With another wave, they walked out into the sunshine with the bag of books swinging gently from the handle of Julia's stroller.

I moved from behind the counter and made my way over to the trio of ladies who'd ended up in the romance section. They were arguing over whether historical or contemporary romances were better and, though I wasn't sure I wanted to get in the middle of that, I figured I should at least welcome them to the store.

Mr. Patterson gestured that he was going to leave and I nodded, smiling my thanks.

"I'll see you on Friday, Little Wynne," he called over the growing din of customers. "Don't forget. I'm treating you to a celebratory dinner at Trudy's."

"I'll be there. Thanks, Mr. Patterson!" I turned back to the ladies. "Now, ladies, why don't you tell me who your favourite authors are and I'll see if I can't find something for each of you."

The morning flew by with a steady stream of curious townspeople coming by to check things out. By two o' clock, I was equal parts overwhelmed, exhilarated and exhausted. I sat down on the tall bar stool I had put behind the counter to save my feet and brushed my long dark hair back from my face. I shuddered to think what it looked like after five hours of absentmindedly raking my hands through it. I'd just kicked off my flats when the door opened and the bell tinkled as Officer Moore walked in. I smiled at her and gestured to the scones and coffee urn.

"Help yourself, Officer Moore, and feel free to browse. Is there anything I can help you find?"

"Call me Sophie, please," she said as she filled a cup with coffee and placed an orange-cranberry scone on the napkin she'd set on the high counter. She leaned on her elbows and smiled. "Can I call you Wynne?"

"Sure," I looked toward the door. "Are the other members of Lake Claire's finest out keeping the peace?"

She grinned and rolled her eyes.

"You guessed it. Black and Mason take themselves pretty seriously and while we were all three about to make our way here, we got a call that there's an altercation happening down at the middle school. They took a squad car and raced over there and

I told them I'd meet them here and represent the Lake Claire Sheriff's Department until they make it."

"You don't seem overly concerned about the fight. Do you know something they don't?" I gave her a quizzical look.

She tossed her head back, laughing. Her brown eyes shone with mirth and I couldn't help grinning at her infectious enthusiasm.

"My friend Jane teaches at the middle school and she told me yesterday when we were having coffee that she overheard two of her students planning a fake fight to impress a couple of girls. I tried to tell Dan and Luke but they insisted that the boys needed to be taught a lesson. I wouldn't be surprised if I find the poor kids sitting in a cell when I get back to the station. Dan takes a pretty hard line on most things and, fake or not, a fighting in the schoolyard is a pet peeve of his. Don't worry, though," she grinned, "I'll spring the boys before Luke has a chance to trump up some charges."

"Well, I said with a shrug, "I suppose it's not a bad thing for them to check it out in case the fake fight gets out of hand. Although," I mused, "I could see Deputy Mason getting them more riled up rather than calming them down. He seems like a man who has something to prove. Sorry." I felt my face flush. "That was unkind.

Sophie studied me, eyes registering her surprise.

"Maybe it was, but you're not wrong. Luke is a bit of a loose cannon at times. I wouldn't be surprised if Dan went along to the school as much to keep him in check as to scare those boys into walking the straight and narrow."

"Even if I was right, I shouldn't have said it. I'm trying to break this nasty habit I have of making quick judgments about people."

I liked Sophie. It was a bit surprising that she'd chosen a career in law enforcement. In some ways, she seemed better suited to something more laid-back and yet – her dark eyes held a deep, steady watchfulness. The combination was intriguing to a people-watcher like me. She lifted a shoulder in an affable shrug.

"It's still a bit of a boy's club in the department, so I may be just as guilty of judging as quickly as you just because I feel like the odd one out." She smiled ruefully. "That's enough about that, though. How about if you show me around your store and talk me into buying something while we get better acquainted? The sheriff and Luke will be here soon."

"I'd love to. What kinds of books do you like best?"

By the time the two men arrived forty-five minutes later, Sophie had a stack of books in her arms and she'd invited me to join her and her friend Jane for brunch on Saturday. The prospect of spending time with single women close to my age made my day. I'd only met her that morning, but already I loved her unvarnished honesty and witty sense of humour. I hoped that she'd become a good friend. I could use as many as I could get.

I started to ring up Sophie's selections while the two men helped themselves to coffee and scones. The sight of a full cash drawer was very welcome after my nervousness that morning. I knew that sales would fluctuate but my first day had already far exceeded my expectations.

"Did you sort out the situation at the school?" I asked as Sheriff Black sipped his coffee.

He gave me a sharp look and then scowled at Sophie.

"I didn't think it was a big secret, Dan," she said calmly. "Schoolyard fights are pretty common."

"I suppose," he allowed grudgingly. "We broke it up and took the boys down the station to cool off. Their parents are coming to pick them up in an hour."

I leaned my elbows on the counter and propped my chin in my hands, noting the smug satisfaction on Deputy Mason's face. Those poor boys were going to get a strip torn off them when their parents arrived, I thought. I just hoped that the parents weren't too hard on them. A quick glance at Sophie told me she was thinking the same thing. I'd bet that she would find a way to tell the parents what her friend overheard and try to keep the consequences from being too severe. I couldn't get a good read on the sheriff, but if it was up to Deputy Mason, I was pretty certain that the boys would be standing in front of a judge tomorrow.

"Well," I cleared my throat lightly, "I certainly do appreciate that you took the time out of your busy day to come to my grand opening. Perhaps you'd like to browse the store to see if there are any books you might be interested in? I have a whole section on true crime if you like something that reminds you of work, or some light fiction if you just want to escape. I've read most of the recent bestsellers so I can give you my opinion on them."

Deputy Mason sidled closer to me as Sophie picked up her bag and walked over to the carafe to refill her coffee cup.

"I wouldn't mind a personal tour, Wynne. Maybe we could start out in the romance section."

He winked and gave me what was probably his most winning smile. All it did was make me wonder how much time it took to keep his teeth so white. He was a good-looking man but everything about him, from his gym-toned muscles to his highlighted hair, seemed fake.

"Why don't I show you and Sheriff Black around together?

If you're interested in the romance section, you can feel free to browse it alone while I show Sheriff Black the rest of the store."

I didn't wait for an answer, but walked from behind the counter forgetting that I wasn't wearing my shoes. I ignored the heat climbing in my cheeks and gestured for the men to follow ne to the true crime section while fending off Deputy Mason's latest attempt at flirtation. When the door opened. and a couple of teenage girls walked in with their mothers. I breathed a sigh of relief and made my way over to them praying that Deputy Mason would take the hint and leave. Much to my delight, he did, but not before sliding his hand down my arm and winking at me as he passed by.

The wave of unease that washed over me reminded me of what I'd felt riding past the Children of the Elements fifteen years earlier. I fought to shrug off the added weight of memory along with the sensation of Deputy Mason's touch. Thankfully, I was distracted by the sound of the bell and the arrival of another round of customers. By the time I flipped the sign from Open to Closed two hours later, I was exhausted. I was also happier than I'd been in a long, long time.

7

Within a couple of weeks, I felt like part of the Lake Claire community and my life settled into a steady routine. After a month, the store was busy enough that I hired a part-time assistant named Jenny Talbot. I'd met her and her electrician husband, Cooper, at church on my second Sunday in town and we'd hit it off right away. They were both a couple of years younger than me and were married only a year ago. Jenny told me that she tried to just keep house for a year and was ready to go crazy. With no kids, and no plans to have any in the near future, she was bored and looking for something to keep her busy and build up their travel fund. I was convinced I'd made a wise business decision in hiring her. She was a gifted saleswoman with a warm manner and love of reading.

I whistled tunelessly as I tied the laces on my running shoes, stretched and slipped my ball cap on. It was just after 6:30am and since it was a Monday, I had a whole free day ahead of me.

I grinned, relishing the contentment that was so surprisingly constant since I'd moved to Lake Claire. I slipped my ear buds in, tucked my iPod into the pocket of my jacket and grabbed the new retractable leash I'd purchased a week ago after a trip to the animal shelter.

"Rochester, come!"

There was a scrabbling sound on the hardwood as the Boston terrier whose big, soulful eyes and adorably ugly face had won my heart at first sight skidded down the hall and slid to an ungainly stop in front of me. I crouched down and rubbed his back while attaching the leash to his collar. The two of us were still getting used to each other but already Rochester was very protective of me. I adored him. He was well-trained and, though not quite fully grown, he had a quiet disposition. He seemed happy to stay near me during the day, had designated himself store security, and spent most of his time observing the proceedings with a dignified air. He was quite affectionate with me but was still weighing others carefully. He'd been abandoned before being brought to the shelter, so I figured that made sense.

I opened the door, led Rochester through and then locked it behind us. Going down the stairs was always an adventure but we managed without either of us tripping this time. The streets were quiet and empty as I walked through town with Rochester at my side. We hit the edge of town in minutes and I let the leash out so that Rochester could run around a bit while I walked at a more even pace. The Jackson house looked as lonely as ever against the summer green of the fields and the grey, cloudy skies. A light breeze blew through the open space, making the grass ripple in a graceful dance.

I'd walked past the Jackson place every day of the two months

I had lived in Lake Claire, always wondering about the family. I knew that it was becoming an obsession but I just couldn't let go. For two months I'd focused on getting my store off the ground and making friends in town. I'd asked a couple of questions about the past, but for the most part, I just hadn't had the time to really focus on finding some answers. The mystery of the abandoned home and the memory of Annie Jackson's dark, frightened eyes, however, still haunted me. I turned around, not allowing myself to walk into the yard or peek in the windows as I always wanted to. The nightmares came with increasing frequency, waking me early at least once a week with cold sweat and a racing heart.

I let the leash out further as Rochester pranced through the grass beside the road, stopping occasionally to investigate whatever took his fancy. Ahead of me, I could see the clearing where the Children of the Elements used to meet for their ceremonies. They used to hold rituals there, many of them by moonlight, or so I'd heard. I stopped next to it and stood for a moment. It looked serene, untouched even, and yet I felt a chill. There was something about the Children of the Elements, though they insisted their goal was love of earth and humanity, that was malignant. It had left a mark. I breathed deep, loving the clean scent of early morning, and told myself firmly that there was nothing to be afraid of here. I walked into the clearing, picked up a stick and threw it for Rochester to fetch. We played for a few minutes, until my arm grew tired, and I set the stick down again.

"Come, Rochester!" I called, turning to leave.

The dog ran past me, brushing my leg, and I stepped sideways to regain my balance. The leash tangled around my ankle and I went down, bringing my arms up to break my fall. I lay for a second on my side to catch my breath as Rochester ran back, nosing my shoulder to see if I was okay.

"I'm fine, boy," I assured him, chuckling ruefully, "and I'm not mad. We'll just chalk this up to mutual clumsiness. We're definitely a match made in heaven."

I rolled onto my back and then sat up, patting my pocket to make sure my phone and keys were still there. Breathing a sigh of relief as I felt them, I leaned forward slightly, ready to get up. My heart nearly stopped as my eyes dropped to the ground between my feet. Blackened by soil and completely devoid of flesh was a foot, and this one definitely did not belong to me. I sucked in a breath, my gasp so loud that Rochester stopped in his tracks on his way toward the road and turned back to see if I was okay.

"Stay, Rochester!"

I scrambled to my feet and walked over to him, grabbing his collar and leading him away from the remains. I retracted the leash and kept him right by my side so he wouldn't be able to investigate the bones and disturb evidence. Reaching into my pocket, I fumbled with my cell phone before retrieving it and taking three tries to punch in 911 with my trembling fingers. I couldn't take my eyes off the bones as I listened to the echoing ringing before the operator answered.

"Yes, my name is Wynne Forrester. I think I've found the remains of a body."

There was no question of whether or not the bones I was staring at were human remains, at least not in my mind. Nonetheless, I thought it prudent to let the police determine that. Unless there were apes running around Lake Claire–other than Luke Mason, that is–the bones had to be human. I gave my location to the operator and assured her that I would stay put until the sheriff arrived. I sank down the grass beside the road, pulling Rochester into my lap and holding him close. He leaned into my arms, stretching his neck so that his face was near mine and licked my chin. I sighed and rubbed my cheek against the top of his head. I sat there silent and staring, my phone still playing though I barely heard it, for what seemed like a lifetime. I checked my watch when I heard the sound of sirens and saw that it was just after seven.

I stood and brushed off my jeans, then reached into my jacket pocket to shut off the music flowing through my ear buds as a single patrol car slowed and pulled onto the approach. I let out the breath I was holding until I saw Sheriff Black and Sophie with him. The last thing I wanted was to deal with Deputy Mason this morning. The two police officers exited their car and walked over to where I stood with Rochester at my side.

"Wynne," said Sheriff Black with a curt nod. "What's this about the remains of a body?"

Sophie's dark eyes met mine; sympathy mingling with shrewdness.

"I was out in the clearing with Rochester playing fetch and taking a break from my walk. We'd just finished and he ran back to the road, bumping me and causing me to lose my footing. I went down and rolled over onto my back. When I sat up and looked down at the ground, I saw the top part of the remains of a foot coming up through the dirt."

"Can you show us where?"

"I'll need to put Rochester in the car first or he'll think it's time to play again."

Sophie opened the back door of the squad car and I told

45

Rochester to hop in, snapping his leash off once he was settled on the back seat.

"I'll be back soon," I murmured, rubbing his soft, silky head.

I shut the door and turned toward the clearing. Less than a minute later, the three of us stood staring down at the macabre sight. Sheriff Black rubbed a hand over his jaw.

"Officer Moore, radio dispatch and have them call in the nearest forensic team available. Before they get here, we need to secure the scene. Miss Roberts, I'm going to need you to stay until the forensic team arrives and can take a sample to exclude your DNA from any trace evidence they find. They'll probably want some fibre comparison samples as well."

I didn't particularly want to stick around any longer but I knew better than to argue. Maybe I'd be able to pick up some information listening as the police and forensic techs consulted with each other. I wanted to ask Sophie or Sheriff Black if they thought the remains might belong to one of the Jacksons but I thought better of it. They probably loved having civilians try to do their jobs as much as I loved anyone telling me what to do. I might be able to convince Sophie to keep me updated but I didn't want to trade on our friendship. If the body did belong to one of the Jacksons, the whole town would know soon enough. I could wait for confirmation. The former worship site of the Children of the Elements as a burial ground was too big a coincidence not to mean something. As queasy as I felt at the discovery in front of me, I recognized a hint of anticipation lurking underneath it. Finally, the secrets of the past might come to light.

The sound of a vehicle approaching drew my attention back to the scene. I watched as a square van pulled off the road onto the approach and parked next to the squad car. Two men emerged wearing jackets that identified them as crime scene techs and walked around to the back of the vehicle to retrieve their kits.

"Hey Dan, Sophie," the older tech, a man who appeared to be in his forties with thinning hair and thick glasses, nodded at each of us in turn. "Is this the young lady who reported the body?"

I waved weakly.

"Wynne Forrester," Sheriff Black said, "this is Dale Brandon and his assistant, Mark Randall. Dale, Mark, this is Wynne. She owns the bookstore that just opened up in Lake Claire and was out walking her dog when she stumbled across what appear to be human remains."

The two men eyed me curiously.

"That will certainly wake you up in a hurry, won't it?"

Mark's face was serious but his blue eyes held a hint of mischief. He was small for a man but the way he held himself suggested boundless energy and a restless nature.

"I think I'd prefer a cup of coffee."

They laughed at my poor attempt at humour as a kindness, I was sure.

"Mark, why don't you go and check out the remains while I collect Miss Forrester's DNA and some fabric samples? Sorry, miss," Dale turned to me, "but I'm going to have cut a small piece off of your jeans and jacket, and take a cheek swab and hair sample."

I smiled at the man as his partner moved further into the field with Sheriff Black and Sophie. He seemed genuinely nice and the worn wedding band on his left ring finger made me feel comfortable with him.

"Do what you need to do, Mr. Brandon. But could you cut the fabric from the knee of my jeans and the elbow of my jacket? Then

I can patch them and still wear them sometimes. As for my hair," I pulled off my ball cap and ran a hand through the sweaty mess, "I need a trim anyway."

He set down his kit, opened it and pulled out what he needed, working quickly. Five minutes later, he was done and I was free to go. It was another five minutes before Rochester was ready, as he was less cooperative with hair and DNA samples than I was. Dale walked over to where his partner was crouched, snapping pictures of the bony foot from every angle and I saw him gesture toward me. Sophie jogged back to where I was standing next to the squad car with Rochester at my side.

"Am I allowed to go home now, Sophie?"

I hated how plaintive I sounded, but I was tired. I just wanted to go back to my apartment, where there were no parts of dead bodies or police watching me carefully. I had no authority or business there, but I felt involved in the case. It was time for some serious searching for answers. Enough is enough with nightmares and regrets; I needed to be free of the past. I was not, however, going to tell Sophie that. It was best for both of us if she didn't know that I planned to do a little information hunting on my own. Her sharp eyes assessed me. It was the first time she'd gone into cop mode with me instead of her laid-back off-duty persona. Looking at her now, I could see the woman who had graduated at the top of her class from the police academy and patrolled dangerous city streets in Chicago.

"Do you want me to drive you back to town, Wynne? Dan won't mind since the techs are going to need quite a bit of time to collect evidence and uncover the body. I'll be back with the car long before he's ready to leave."

"No, Sophie, you stay here. The walk will do me good." I

wondered if I was going to be able to sleep tonight. Already, I had formed a mental image of the whole skeleton with the skull, huge empty eye sockets and all, grinning at me. "It won't take me more than twenty minutes to get back to my place."

She gave me a critical look, and I felt myself wilting.

"You look pale. Hang on a sec," she commanded before turning and running back to where the men were standing. Barely a minute passed before she was back by the car.

"Come on. I'm walking you home. My shift will be over in less than an hour and I'm not needed here. Dan agreed that it would be a good idea for me to make sure you get home safe, and then head to the station and fill Luke in before I go off duty."

It seemed like too much work to argue with her, so I just nodded and started walking back toward town. I barely noticed her presence as we moved down the road. I remembered everything I'd heard about the cult and the Jackson family. There had to be records of their disappearance in the town newspaper archives and I could do an online search to see if the Children of the Elements were operating somewhere else or were well and truly disbanded. I picked up my pace, re-energized at the prospect of satisfying my curiosity.

"You look a little better already, Wynne. Walking was a good idea."

I glanced sideways at Sophie. I'd forgotten she was there, but she was easily keeping up with me, arms swinging loosely at her sides.

"Yeah, I needed the air and exercise to clear my head. Sophie," I hesitated, and then went with impulse. "Do you think the body could belong to one of the Jacksons?"

She looked at me warily, eyes guarded.

"It's too early to speculate. What makes you ask?"

I was about to explain my theory and the reasons behind it when I caught myself. If I told Sophie that I'd been haunted by the family's disappearance for the last fifteen years, I'd lose all credibility along with any faith she had in my objectivity. Besides, I'd just promised myself not to involve her in my plans.

"Well, they're the only people who've disappeared from around here. I thought it made sense that the body might belong to one of them."

"That does seem logical. I suppose we'll find out soon enough."

"How long will it take?"

"It depends on the lab and how backlogged they are. At least getting DNA to compare that of the remains to won't be a problem since it's already in the system."

I stopped, surprised.

"Why is it in the system already? When did that happen?"

She winced.

"I probably shouldn't have said anything about that but I suppose it doesn't matter too much. When the family disappeared fifteen years ago, investigators took the precaution of collecting their hairbrushes and toothbrushes. They wanted to be prepared in case they ever had bodies to compare it to. I'm not sure if any samples they can pull will still be viable, but there's a chance."

"Smart of them to do that – was Sheriff Black already sheriff back then? He's been in town for quite a few years, hasn't he?"

"I'm not sure. He worked his way up the ranks, so he was probably still a deputy fifteen years ago." She grinned suddenly. "Funny, huh? Sheriff Black was working his way up in the force and you and I doing our best to make it through middle school unscathed. Sometimes I forget how much younger I am than him."

I laughed humorlessly.

"I think he managed his end of things better than I did. 'Unscathed' does not exactly describe my psyche during or after middle school."

She shot me a commiserating look.

"Mine either. I'd just changed schools and was incredibly shy. I spent most of my time with my cousins. They were good-looking, athletic and, worst of all, genuinely nice."

"Isn't that the worst? Let me guess, you felt insecure, unappealing and inferior."

"In spades."

I smiled fully for the first time since I'd made my grisly find.

"I guessed we were kindred spirits, Sophie, but I think that proves it."

"I don't know if I should consider that a compliment or not."

As we entered the outskirts of town, I felt myself relax and the morning's horror receded. For the moment.

8

By the time I'd showered, dressed, and fed Rochester, Sophie was back from the station and knocking at my door.

"Are you ready for breakfast?"

She'd changed out of her uniform and looked fresh and relaxed in a magenta t-shirt and faded jeans. Her thick, dark hair was pulled back in a high ponytail. If I didn't know that she'd just come off a night shift, I would have sworn she had gotten a solid eight hours of sleep, she looked so rested. If I didn't enjoy her company so much, that would have been enough to make me dislike the woman on principle. People who bounce out of bed and into calisthenics or work nights and come away looking dewy fresh are the bane of my existence. My mind wakes quickly, but the rest of me doesn't catch up for at least an hour. I pity anyone who encounters me before brain and body are in sync.

"I think so. Rochester, be good," I called over my shoulder before shutting the door and locking it.

"So, am I allowed to talk to anyone about what I found this morning?"

"Well," she drew the word out, "the sheriff can't stop you. In a town this size, rumours are probably already circulating. We had to pass the Kincaid place on our way to the clearing and you know how Mrs. Kincaid likes to gossip. By the time we get to Trudy's, everyone there will probably know more than we do."

I grinned and lifted my face to the clean breeze that tousled my hair. Though I would have preferred to start this morning without stumbling over a corpse, it was still a beautiful day.

"Is my interest in finding out whose body I tripped over and what happened going to hurt our friendship, Sophie? I'd hate to lose that–I really would–but I don't think I can leave this alone."

I held my breath as I waited for her answer. Sophie shook her head firmly, smiling easily, and I felt my shoulders relax.

"I'm not going to resent you or be angry if you ask a few questions, Wynne, but I want you to be careful. Sheriff Black is another story, and so is Deputy Mason. Neither of them is going to be happy with your involvement, and I can't afford to take your part with them."

"I know that and I don't expect it from you. I just wanted to make sure that we're still good."

I pushed open the door to Trudy's and gestured her in ahead of me. Dot saw us immediately and motioned that we should pick whichever spot we wanted to sit. We both made a beeline for our usual table by the window and made ourselves comfortable while we waited for Dot to make her way to us with the coffeepot. She hurried toward us in less than a minute, face alight with curiosity.

"Well, girls, I hear you've had quite the morning. That must have been quite a shock for you, Wynne."

A laugh bubbled up and out of my throat.

"Dot, how on earth do you know about what happened this morning already? The sheriff hasn't even made it back to the station, and I know for a fact that Sophie didn't say anything yet."

The older woman smiled, feline satisfaction glimmering in her bright green eyes.

"Didn't you know that Charlie's got a police scanner in the kitchen, Wynne? He hears everything that goes on in this town as soon as it happens and what doesn't cross those wavelengths I collect from customers in here. It's a no-fail system."

"That's incredible!"

I was impressed and a little intimidated.

"Do I want to know what you know about me?"

Dot's grin was unrepentant.

"Probably not, but if you ever have any questions about yourself, just come find me and I'll fill you in. You girls want your usual?"

We both nodded, and she scurried off to the kitchen to tell the cook.

The restaurant was only about half full, so we were able to talk easily without having to raise our voices to be heard.

"Sophie, I'm sorry to keep harping on this but I really want to know. Do you think it's likely that the body is one of the Jacksons? I realize you don't have forensics yet but give me your gut feeling."

She sighed and propped her chin on her hands, eyes far away as she thought. After a minute, she met my gaze.

"I think it is," she said quietly so that she wouldn't be overheard. "It makes the most sense of anything else I've thought of."

I blew out a breath.

"That's what I thought too." I sat back slightly and crossed my arms. "After breakfast, I'm going straight to the library archives to look up newspapers from around the time the Jackson family disappeared. Maybe there's something in there that can help me figure out what happened."

Sophie looked like she was about to say something, but Dot arrived with our food. We both dug in and ate in silence for a while before turning to lighter topics. After finishing our breakfasts amidst a heated debate over the best leading men from classic movies, we waved goodbye to Dot and went our separate ways. Sophie went home to bed since was working another night shift later on, and I went straight to the library.

The Lake Claire Public Library is mid-way down a side street just off Main. I walked the few blocks from Trudy's to the old brick building that had housed the town archives and lending library since the late 19th century. Every time I walked through the thick wooden doors and into the large, airy main room I breathed in deep at the smell leather binding. If I ever doubted that I was an incurable bibliophile, the smell of old books was the only reminder I'd need. Public libraries were deadly for my back but better for my wallet than bookstores, since the large bags of books I inevitably toted home were heavy but free.

The old building was quiet and empty. Since it was a beautiful day, most people chose to enjoy the weather instead of wandering through stacks of books. I, on the other hand, had never found sunny days particularly appealing. My pale skin doesn't tan, so my options are SPF 45 and a broad brimmed hat or a nice red sunburn that doesn't fade until fall is well underway. Rainy days and books suit me down to the ground.

There were internet stations that allowed access to the national newspaper archives, but I bypassed them in favour of the archive room with its old microfiche machine. Larger newspapers wouldn't have the small town gossip that the *Lake Claire Gazette* did. I already knew the basic details of the disappearance; what I wanted was public opinion. I scrolled through various editions, starting with the Society section and Community Events from every weekend edition of the year prior to the Jackson family disappearance. I wanted to see if there was some indication of who the members of the Children of the Elements were. If I cross-referenced community events involving Mara Prentice and Mitchell Lawrence, priestess and priest of the Children of the Elements, business partners and lovers, with the movements of families featured in the Society pages, I might get a better picture of just who else was involved in their group.

I leaned over, reached into my bag and pulled out a notebook and pen. Within an hour, I had a page full of names of people involved in at least the fringes of cult activity. The fact that the majority of my list was comprised of doctors, lawyers, business owners and well-placed town officials came as no surprise to me, but I was cynical by nature. Any group seeking power would naturally cultivate intimacy with those in town who already held it. Power by proxy is a long-standing method of gaining control.

The front paper of the first edition released following the Jacksons' disappearance was devoted to an article about the previous week's town meeting. The disappearance was finally mentioned on the third page in a frustratingly vague article that said there was an ongoing investigation. The writer, Ellis Porter, had done nothing more than the bare minimum.

The name seemed familiar so I dropped my eyes to the list I'd set on the desk next to me. Sure enough, there it was in my own clear writing–Ellis Porter. I'd made a little notation next to each name of the date of the paper it was found in and which even connected to it. My notes showed that Ellis Porter had been the reporter of record for every event the Children of the Elements hosted and had praised them liberally. It was not conclusive proof of his involvement with them, but it was enough for me. The way he glossed over the Jackson family's disappearance was just another weight on that scale.

After scanning the following month of papers and finding nothing more of value I shut down the microfiche machine and stuffed my notebook and pen into my bag before heading out of the archive room. A quick glance showed me the library was still empty, so I settled in at an internet station, typing in my library card number. A search of the latest *Lake Claire Gazette* issue online revealed that Ellis Porter was still alive, well and reporting. In fact, he was now the paper's editor-in-chief.

As I pushed the heavy wooden door of the library open, I wondered how I was going to get the information I wanted from a reporter who was once–and possibly still was–-very loyal to people I suspected of murder. I wasn't comfortable with outright lying and had a terrible poker face anyway. Winging it seemed my best option. If all else failed, my blunt questions might fluster the man enough to make him reveal something useful. I quickened my steps as I headed down the sidewalk toward the newspaper office. I hoped that I would end up with more truth than trouble, but in all likelihood, I was probably headed for both.

9

The *Lake Claire Gazette* was a small paper and, judging from the by-lines, bursting with nepotism. In the most recent editions of the paper, the front page articles were written by Cassandra Porter and Ellis Porter, Jr. The paper was obviously a family affair with Ellis Porter, Sr. as editor, and I wondered if the relatives–Ellis, Jr. had to be Ellis, Sr.'s son and third Porter on staff was too big a coincidence not to be some sort of family–were involved with the Children of the Elements or not. If they were both working at the paper, these two wanted to please Ellis, Sr., so it was more than possible.

The large glass door opened easily when I pushed at it. The lobby was noisier than I'd expected for a small town paper. The phone was ringing, and a young woman stabbed away at her computer keyboard energetically. The sound of raised voices from the editor's office filtered through the din. I looked around for a receptionist, but the front desk was empty. I eased my way forward until I could decipher the shouting, trying not to look as conspicuous as I felt. The young woman took no notice of me, so I must have been succeeding, and I wandered closer to the editor's office.

"What do you mean you won't run it? This is the biggest story to hit Lake Claire for years! I had to promise Mark Crandall two great tickets to the next home game in the city to get that shot of the skeleton, along with dinner for two at Giovanni's to Deputy Mason for an "undisclosed source". This is real news! It's not another article on town council and whether or not Main Street needs traffic lights!"

"It's all hearsay. Distasteful hearsay at that. ! Lake Claire is a peaceful town and people do not want their home soiled by something as sordid as a murder. Now, I will run an edited version of your article on page two or three, wherever there's room, but the photo is out!"

"I can't believe you're doing this, Uncle Ellis!" Uncle, I thought. Interesting. And the man's voice ruled Cassandra Porter out as the speaker. I leaned closer, intrigued. "Oh wait; I just remembered who I'm talking to. For the man who has single-handedly policed the news for almost twenty years, brushing one measly murder victim under the carpet is nothing! What you do is an abuse of your position!"

"How dare you! How dare you say that after everything I've done for you! When your parents died twenty years ago, I could have let you go into foster care. Your aunt and I gave you a home out of the goodness of our hearts, fed you, clothed you and sent you to school. Then, when you got it into your foolish head that you wanted to make a living as a photographer, I even gave you a job here at the paper so you at least had a steady pay check!"

"You let me live in your house but you never gave me a home! Don't insult me by pretending you or Aunt Barbara cared for me at all or that I owe you anything." I inched ever closer. I didn't want to interrupt the shouting match and have that fury turned on me. Besides, I might be able to learn some of what I wanted to know without even having to ask.

The younger voice continued. "I talked to my parent's lawyer when I was sixteen, and he told me that there was a trust set up. He sent you money from it every month for my care, five hundred dollars for necessities and an extra five hundred for you as my guardians. He never told you that there was another fund for my education. My mother knew you well enough to know that if you found out about it, you'd try to find a way to take that too. She was right, wasn't she? All of those years I went to school in clothes from the thrift store while your wife and children went around in designer labels, the vacations you took after shipping me off to summer camp were financed by my parent's life insurance payouts!"

"You can't prove any of that! You're just bitter! You were a disturbed boy and now you're a seriously unstable man!"

I waited, holding my breath, for a furious retort but it didn't come. Instead, after a pause, the second voice spoke almost calmly. "I was bitter, Uncle, and I still fight that. It's taken me a long time to forgive you and Aunt Barbara for what you did. I thought that if I accepted your offer to work here, things could change between us. I want to be gracious but I can't stay on here. You distort the truth for your own purposes, and I won't be a part of that. I'm quitting. You should know that I've decided to start another paper for Lake Claire; one that prints the truth. The papers are ready to sign for my office space, but I wanted to give you one final chance to do the right thing. Since you refuse to print my pictures or anything about the body that was found I'll cover it in my inaugural edition, and I'll do under my own name, not yours."

The door swung open and I stepped back, trying to look occupied with studying the framed copies of newspapers hanging on the wall. The man walking out was tall, about six feet, and tanned with the kind of deep natural colour that comes from years of summers out of doors. His dark brown hair was a bit shaggy with golden lights in it. His eyes that widened in surprise at the sight of my eavesdropping self lurking right outside the door were a deep green. He started to say something, but the irate voice from inside the room cut him off.

"You'll never make a go of it, Noah! Nobody in this town will trust you or a thing you print!"

Noah winced but said nothing as he closed the office door behind him. He glanced at me with a questioning look. I offered my hand, smiling tentatively.

"Hello, I'm Wynne Forrester. I thought perhaps somebody here could tell me something about whose body was found this morning but I guess, after overhearing that, it won't be your uncle. He doesn't seem terribly interested in the details."

"That would be the understatement of the year," he said, blowing out a long breath as he glanced toward the closed door.

"Well, you see, I have a personal interest in the case and I'd like to find out any new details."

"What kind of interest?"

"I sort of found the body."

His eyes widened and he grabbed my arm, hurrying me toward the front door.

"Come on. I know somewhere we can talk."

He stopped only to retrieve a camera bag and leather satchel hanging from the back of a desk chair. He waved over his shoulder at the woman still engrossed in her typing, but she was oblivious to our leaving. He pushed the door open and led me out into the sunny afternoon. I kept pace with his long strides, saying nothing as we walked first one, then two and then three blocks at a steady clip.

It wasn't until the old gas station at the edge of town came into view that he slowed a bit and seemed to realize that he still had my arm in his grasp.

"Sorry about that," he said sheepishly as he relaxed his grip. "I didn't mean to manhandle you. I was just so intent on getting away from my uncle and finding a place where I could interview you in private that I kind of acted without thinking."

I shrugged and tried not to blush. I wasn't comfortable with men, and the one holding my arm was both strong and attractive. He wasn't handsome, but his features were pleasing. It was the intensity in his eyes that set him apart and made me want to know if he felt strongly about everything or if he chose his passions carefully.

"It's all right. I like a good, brisk walk. Actually, that's how I ended up finding the body. Not that walking with you is like finding a dead body," I said and then winced at the inanity of my comment. "I mean to say... Never mind, I don't think I can recover after that."

His laugh rang out; a deep rumble that made it impossible not to smile back.

"I'm not at all offended, Miss Forrester. I think that we're going to get along very well. I thought so the very first time I saw you looking all flustered one morning at Trudy's." His smile widened as a flush crept up my neck over the memory of Grandpa's matchmaking attempt with Deputy Mason. Then he asked, "Now, what do you say I buy us both something to drink, and we go sit in the park while you tell me all about what happened this morning?"

"I say yes, but you can call me Wynne. And be forewarned. I have some questions for you as well. I guess the first one is rather obvious. Who are you?"

"I'm Noah Sutton, but please, call me Noah. I was the photographer for the *Lake Claire Gazette*, but I'm striking out on my own as of today. Now, what kind of soda would you like?"

"A Diet Coke, please, and I'll wait outside, if you don't mind. If I see five-cent candies, I'm going to want some and I don't need the sugar rush."

"Done. I'll be just a minute."

He shot me a quick smile, let go of my arm and headed into the gas station. I walked over to an empty parking space and sat on the edge of the sidewalk. Leaning forward, I propped my elbows on my knees and dropped my chin into my hands. The sun was warm on my back; comforting. I couldn't figure out which thing made the churning in my stomach–spending time alone with a good-looking man, or the memory of skeletal remains etched into my brain.

I jerked my head up as I heard the sound of the door opening. Noah walked toward me with two bottles, one in either hand and offered me the Diet Coke.

"Thanks. So, are you ready to head to the park?"

"Absolutely; lay on, MacDuff!"

I started toward the park, turning to grin at Noah as he fell in step with me.

"Fan of Macbeth, are we?"

"With the family I come from, Wynne, you have no idea how normal Shakespearean plays make me feel."

He smiled back at me and I felt my grin grow wider.

"I think, Noah," I said, feeling more at ease than I would have thought possible five minutes before, "that you're absolutely right. We're going to get along just fine."

10

It took less than ten minutes for us to reach the small park near the centre of Lake Claire. We bypassed the wooden bench beside the walking path in favour of the old swing set. It was the same one that I'd played on during my summers with my grandparents, though the wooden seats had been replaced with plastic ones. The round tire I used to spin on until I could hardly see straight was still there, and I smiled at the memories it sparked. I walked past it to a single swing, and Noah plopped down on the one next to it. The steeple of Lake Claire Community Church was visible through the tall trees at the edge of the playground, and I studied it as I sipped at my Diet Coke. Memories of my childhood summers flitted through my mind. I was so lost in my own thoughts that I jumped, nearly spilling my drink, when Noah spoke.

"So tell me, Wynne; how does exactly does one go about finding a skeleton first thing in the morning?"

I pushed my feet into the ground to start my swing moving.

"I would venture a guess that it's different for everyone," I said dryly, "but I happened to be playing with Rochester, when he bumped into me and I fell down. As I sat up, I looked around and saw three feet pointing up near the ends of my legs; my two and one skeletal specimen sticking out of the ground between them."

"Did you scream?"

I shot him a withering look. "I don't remember but I don't think so. I'm hardly the type of woman who faints at the sight of blood–or bones, in this case. It did shake me up quite a bit, though. I'll admit that."

"That doesn't surprise me. Anybody would be shaken up, if they stumbled across something like that. I didn't mean to offend you when I asked if you screamed." Deep green eyes studied me for a moment, a hint of mischief glimmering in them. "I only asked because I'm pretty sure I would have shrieked like a little girl before running away."

I felt myself relax a bit more at the quick, honest answer, a grin tugging at my lips at the mental picture.

"Sorry I got snarky. I tend to assume people see the worst in me, since that's what I see, and it makes me defensive."

"I understand, Wynne. It's okay."

I met his gaze and realized, to my surprise, that he actually did understand. Flustered, I looked out at the trees again and took another sip of my soda. We sat that way for a while, swings rocking gently back and forth, both of us lost in our thoughts.

"Can I ask you something, Noah?" At his nod, I continued. "Were you in Lake Claire when the Jackson family disappeared? I'm asking because I remember it. I spent summers here with my grandparents growing up, and I've never felt easy about the way everybody just wrote them off. Now that a body has turned up, I just need to know more."

His expression was open, so I tried to explain further.

"It's not like I have some conspiracy theory or something," I said. "Well, actually, yes it is. Forget I just said that. I think their disappearance had something to do with their involvement in the Children of the Elements. I saw them in that same clearing–the one where I found the body–on the last day they were seen. There was some sort of ceremony happening as I rode past on my bike. I used to go out and look at the Jackson place all the time. Something about it made me feel..." I searched for the right word, "akin to it, I suppose. I didn't really have anybody who understood me back then. but that house felt like a friend."

I often assigned human characteristics to houses and objects. I saw all manner of emotions in the things around me though, and I couldn't help personifying them. I was expecting at least a hint of mockery in Noah's face, and I steeled myself not to get hurt. Almost everyone made fun of me over it. The conspiratorial grin that flashed across his face was entirely unexpected and I felt my heart warm.

"I thought I was the only kid who used to sneak out to the Jackson place for comfort. That old house made me feel a lot less lonely. I identified with it, and that was a feeling I certainly never had in my uncle's house. I'm surprised we never bumped into each other there. I used to go every evening after supper." His look turned wry. "My summer days usually consisted of either working on my aunt and uncle's house–painting and other repairs–or working a summer job since I had to pay for my own clothing, shoes and everything else."

My distaste for his aunt and uncle must have shown on my face, because he chuckled and gave a slight shrug as if to say it didn't matter anymore. Right, I thought, sure it doesn't.

"That explains it," I replied with a laugh. "My grandparents never allowed me out after supper unless they were with me. They were afraid I'd get mugged or something. It wasn't so bad until I finished college and spent a full ten days here instead of the one or two I usually did. By then, I figured I should be able to go for an evening stroll alone without it turning into a battleground at home. I was wrong about that. We managed to keep our relationship intact, but it was dicey for a bit."

"Who are your grandparents? I know most everyone in town, at least by reputation."

"Their names are Jim and Rose Newton. Grandpa used to be a carpenter before he retired and Grandma was busy with the kids, then grandkids, baking and keeping the household running well."

Noah laughed, his eyes dancing with mischief.

"I know Jim Newton very well, indeed. Perhaps you remember a time about ten years back when he and his brothers decided to enter themselves as a team in the annual amateur curling competition?"

I nodded, grinning at the memory of the four stubborn men and their muttered complaints about each other as they played. It had been far more entertaining than the actual game.

"Well, I was taking a year to work after high school so I could save some money for college. I not only bagged groceries; I mowed lawns and shovelled sidewalks and, best of all, I drove the Zamboni for the rink. That's where I met your grandfather and later, your grandma when she brought her pies and buns for the farmer's market. My stomach has never forgiven me for introducing it to her baking and then not keeping up the acquaintance. I don't suppose she taught you her secrets in the kitchen?"

I burst out laughing at the hopeful expression on his face.

"Maybe she did and maybe she didn't. I'll let you wonder for a while."

"You're heartless, Wynne!"

"I know it."

He nudged my shoulder companionably as he swung gently against me.

"I'd like to be your friend, Wynne." I blinked at his frankness, but decided it was a refreshing change from beating around the bush. "I'm glad I met you today, even if the circumstances weren't ideal. I moved home to Lake Claire about six months ago and haven't really managed to carve out much of a personal life. Most of my school friends are grown and gone, and I've been spending my free weekends travelling to visit university buddies."

"Let me guess. It's a great time while you're there, but you come home and end up a loner again because you haven't really put down roots here. Then, because you're lonely, you make plans to go away again on your next free weekend and the cycle continues.

He laughed again and nodded.

"That about sums it up. I've been trying to decide which church to attend and even that has me running scared. I tried out Lake Claire Community and felt more comfortable than I thought I would, but still..." He let the sentence hang.

"Why are you so nervous? Just attending doesn't mean you're locked in, does it?"

"Wynne," Noah's face was a picture of long-suffering amusement, "I was taken in and raised, if you can call it that, by an aunt and uncle who were cult members. Why do you think I'm afraid of churches?"

"I see your point. But what's drawing you to it, if you find it so intimidating?"

He leaned back, tilting his head so he could study the clouds while he formulated his answer. After a minute, he pushed off with his legs again and let himself swing back and forth a few times before turning back to me and meeting my eyes.

"My folks were really great people. When they died together in a car accident on the way home from celebrating their fifteenth wedding anniversary, I wanted to die too. I was only eleven. I was so angry at God for letting it happen and for making me live with my aunt and uncle. Before the accident I'd been a pretty good kid and loved attending services with my parents but after they died, I was ready to walk away–except I couldn't bear the thought of disappointing my mother, even if she was gone. After about six months, I realized that I wasn't angry with God anymore. I needed somebody to look out for me and love me and from what I'd learned from my folks, God already did. The next day after school I walked over to the nearest church. It was the Anglican one, which is now Lake Claire Community, and asked the priest for a Bible."

He gestured at the steeple that was visible through the trees and then dropped his hand to his side. I tried to picture him as a boy, serious and sad-eyed on the doorstep of an old, worn church, and my heart broke a little.

"What did he say?"

"Not much at first," he smiled as his eyes took on a faraway look. "He just told me to follow him into his office, pulled a nice, new leather Bible out of a desk drawer, handed it to me and asked if I wanted any help figuring it out."

"Did you?"

"Not really at that point but I didn't want to be rude, so I said maybe. I told him that I almost always had chores on the weekends so I couldn't come to church. I thought that would be the end of his interest in me. Instead, before I really know what was happening, I'd agreed to come and talk over whatever I read after school every Thursday. By the time I was in high school, he was the closest thing to a father I had. Our visits are the best memories I have since before my parents died. I went off to college knowing I had one person here that would miss me, pray for me and be happy to see me when I came home again."

His eyes were dark with memory and I couldn't help putting a hand on his arm as I spoke.

"I'm sure he counted himself blessed to have you in his life as well. How could he not?"

Noah shook his head as though to clear the past from his thoughts.

"He always made a point of telling me so. When the diocese decided to close down the church, he called me and told me that he was going to have to move. He was hoping it wouldn't be too far from Lake Claire. He knew I planned to come back here eventually."

"Where's he living now? Is he one of the friends you've been visiting on weekends?"

"Father Bryce moved into a senior's complex called Piny Ridge about an hour south of here. One of his oldest friends, Mr. Patterson, lives there as well and from what the father tells me the two of them have their hands full fighting off the female population."

I burst out laughing.

"Did he seriously tell you that? I've heard that retirement communities are worse than university dorms but I didn't quite believe it."

Noah nodded soberly but couldn't hide the twinkle in his eyes.

"Actually, last time we talked on the phone he said that he had to go because the lawn bowling tournament was starting soon and he had promised Mr. Patterson he'd be his wingman."

"He didn't actually use the term 'wingman', did he?"

"I nearly passed out from the shock but yes, he did. When I asked him where he heard that phrase, he told me if I didn't know what it meant he felt sorry for me and I needed to get a life."

I nearly fell off my swing, I was laughing so hard. The gleam of my watch caught my eye and I automatically checked the time. I could hardly believe that Noah and I had been sitting in the park for as long as we had.

"I hate to say this but I have to leave. Rochester needs his supper and I've got some things I need to take care of today since the shop is open for the rest of the week. Thanks for the Diet Coke and conversation. I had a great time." I paused and then tried to sound casual. "Maybe I'll see you at church on Sunday."

My heart tripped a little at the obvious disappointment in Noah's eyes. I'd never seen that look directed at me by a man before and I suddenly suspected I could be a very silly female with little provocation. I started to push myself out of my swing, afraid of what I was feeling. I liked Noah Sutton. I liked him a lot and I wanted him to like me...a lot.

"Wait, Wynne, let me walk you home. We barely got to scratch the surface of the whole mess surrounding the body you discovered this morning. Maybe we could get together again soon? We could be unofficial investigative partners. You can gather public opinion at your bookstore. I'll print whatever we find out, if we can verify it. Besides," he smiled and it made his eyes crinkle at the corners, "I like talking with you."

"When were you thinking?"

"Well," he fell easily into step with me despite the heavy camera equipment he still carried, "I also have some things I have to do today, unfortunately. What about tomorrow? What time do you open the shop?"

"I'm there by nine. I also walk every morning at about 6:30."

"Would you mind some company on your morning walk?" He smiled again. "I'll even buy you breakfast afterward."

I felt my face flush and I had to fight to keep from skipping.

"I'd like that."

We walked silent, side by side, turning toward my apartment.

"Wynne?"

"Yes, Noah?"

"Who's Rochester? Should I be worried that you're hurrying home to make his supper?"

My laugh echoed down the street as we turned and headed toward my apartment. I'd have to fill him in on how little a threat Rochester was, but for now I was just going to enjoy the fact that Noah was interested enough to ask if I belonged to another man or not. It had been a long time since I'd felt the stirring of hope that my future might include someone to walk alongside me through life. I wasn't going to pin my dreams on Noah–it was definitely too early to feel anything more than attraction–but, maybe, it was time to try opening my heart to what could be.

II

Twisted tree branches loomed black against the bright morning sky. Sunlight so intense it burned my eyes illuminated the ground in front of me. My chest hurt and I gasped for air but every breath only served to pull more oxygen out of me as it was expelled. I was sweaty; I'd been running so hard that my stomach revolted. I looked around, frantically searching for Rochester but he was gone. I stepped forward, ready to call for him, when I tripped over something protruding from the ground. I stumbled, dropping to my hands and knees. Staring up at me was a skull; hollow features macabre and menacing. A scream rose up in my throat as black spots danced across my vision, meeting to form a dark void that stole my consciousness. Just before I fainted, a soft, querulous voice called from the ground beneath me.

"Wait! There's something I need to tell you! You have to know..."

My eyes flew open. It was dark. A glance at my alarm clock showed that it was only quarter after five. My sheets were twisted and tangled about me, evidence of my restless sleep. There was no sense in lying uncomfortably for the half hour before I had to get up anyway, so I rolled over and pushed myself up without disturbing Rochester's sleeping form at the foot of my bed. At least my dog, if his snuffling snores were any indication, was getting a good rest.

I wandered into the kitchen and hit the on button on the coffee maker so it could perk while I showered and dressed. I'd be having breakfast with Noah in just a couple of hours and I wanted to look nice, and awake. After a quick shower, I hurried through my bare minimum make-up routine and blow-dried my hair. I said a heartfelt prayer of thanks when my dark brown hair fell into its chin-length bob with very little coaxing. It might not be important in the grand scheme of things, but I never took a good hair day for granted. Besides, an excuse to be thankful was never a bad thing. I could see shadows under my eyes from my poor sleep but they weren't too noticeable.

I hoped.

The dark blue jeans I pulled on were stylishly snug, the color contrasting nicely with my thigh-length cream top. The boat neckline flattered me, and I thought the silvery-blue of the camisole peeking through the holes in the crocheted sweater made my eyes look more luminous than usual. The high flush in my cheeks was definitely a result of the prospect of seeing Noah again. I wondered if I was setting myself up for disappointment but squashed the thought. The niggling uncertainty in my heart was an old friend I was determined to ignore.

The barest hint of grey dawn was visible through my bedroom window as I walked back into the room.

"Come on, Rochester! Time to get up so I can make my bed and have a little snack before Noah gets here."

One sleepy brown eye opened and gave me a disparaging look. I snickered and he lifted his head to glare at me. The effect was ruined by the fact that one side of his face was squished in from lying on it all night. I burst out laughing and picked him up for a quick cuddle before placing him on the floor.

"I know, I know," I said, looking back as I smoothed and tucked in covers, "your mistress is so cruel, making you wake up so early and then laughing at you. It's a rough life, isn't it?"

I received a baleful look as he shuffled out of the bedroom and into the kitchen in search of his own breakfast. His mood would improve when he saw me pick up his leash. I finished smoothing the covers in time to the lilting sounds of Celtic music I'd turned on in my living room. I gave my bed a final pat and then walked into the kitchen, poured myself a mug of coffee and breathed in the distinctive aroma. I savored the first sip before setting down my mug and grabbing an apple from the fridge. A glance at the clock showed I still had fifteen minutes before Noah was due to arrive, so I pared the fruit and put apple slices in a small bowl. I leaned against the counter and watched the sky lighten through the kitchen window, munching on the apple slices and sipping my coffee.

By five to six, I was ready to go. Instead of my usual hooded sweatshirt, I took out my grey plaid coat. It wasn't quite as warm, but I wanted to look put together. I'd chosen my outfit this morning with my walking companion very much in mind, and it was a definite change from my usual yoga pants and hooded jacket. My concession to comfort was the pair of running shoes instead of dress flats. If I was going to walk a fair distance, I needed to be practical about that, at least. I'd just taken Rochester's leash from its hook next to the door when I heard a knock.

"Just a second," I called, quickly clipping the leash to the dog's collar, "I'll be right there."

Making sure I had a good grip on Rochester's leash, I patted my coat pocket to check if my keys were there and then opened the door. Noah had on a pair of dark, distressed jeans and a leather jacket zipped all the way up to keep out the cool morning breeze. I was relieved that I wasn't overdressed and secretly hoped he had wanted to look nice for me too. I wasn't going to ask, since I didn't want to assume he was as interested in me as I was in him. I hoped I was adult enough not to stress over that, but I was overwhelmingly aware that being female meant fighting the constant battle against personal drama.

"Hi Noah," I said as I walked through the doorway and tugged it closed behind me. Instead of making his usual headlong dash for the stairs, Rochester wandered over to Noah and sniffed his feet. Huffing out his breath, the dog lay down, rolled over and offered his stomach for rubbing. Noah laughingly obliged while I locked the door.

"Sorry about that," I gestured to the reclining form of my dog who was groaning with eyes half-shut in pleasure. "He's not very subtle. Rochester, show some pride, would you?"

All I got for my comment was a disdainful look from my pet and an amused one from Noah.

"I don't think he's too concerned with his dignity, Wynne." Noah gave him a final pat on the belly before straightening.

"Fine, then," I said nonchalantly, jingling the leash as I moved toward the stairs, "I guess I'll just go for a walk by myself. Bye, Rochester."

My foot hadn't even hit the first step before Rochester scrambled to his feet and raced ahead of me. He was nearly to the bottom of the stairs when the leash pulled him up short, and he was forced to wait impatiently while Noah and I caught up. We fell into an easy rhythm, my brisk strides matching Noah's pace despite the fact that his legs were even longer than mine. I savored the simple pleasure of walking with someone that was matched me step for step. Most women were shorter than me and nearly had to jog to keep up, and, my dad and brothers were all the kind of men who moseyed–if they walked at all.

"You look a bit tired this morning, Wynne. Didn't you sleep well?"

Inordinate pleasure that Noah had noticed swelled before it was quashed by the realization that if he had, I definitely didn't look my best. What if I had traces of apple in my teeth too? Self-conscious at the thought, I surreptitiously slid my tongue across them to check before answering, thinking that I was nearly as undignified as my dog. Cue the drama, I thought wryly.

"Not especially," I answered, pulling my thoughts back to his question. "I had a bit of a nightmare, so I got up earlier than I'd planned."

"I'm sorry to hear it. I'm not surprised, though. You did stumble across human remains yesterday. That's enough to give anyone nightmares."

I nodded and tilted my head to look at him while Rochester wandered happily along ahead of us.

"Have you heard anything further about who it was and how he or she died?"

"Not much. The sheriff's department is pretty close-mouthed about ongoing investigations, and they really hate it when they think someone is poking in where they don't belong."

"That's not surprising," I said with a frown. "I suppose I might feel that way too. But, wouldn't they want to use every avenue available to make an identification and figure out what happened? I guess I'm idealistic enough to think that egos shouldn't get in the way of finding answers."

"You wouldn't believe some of the stuff I ran into when I was interning as a photographer for a major paper–cops who showboated, reporters who never checked facts and even lied outright just for a good story. There were some really solid people on both sides–the majority of law enforcement and journalists, actually–but a few rotten ones gave us all a bad name and it was hard when there was such baggage attached to the job. As soon as I finished university, I decided I needed a break from it all. I was fortunate enough to find studio work that paid well right away. After a couple of years, I'd saved enough to travel around Europe, Africa and parts of Asia with my camera and a backpack. I sent my shots back to a university friend who worked at a publishing house. He's a natural salesman and managed to convince the powers that be to take a look at them. The next thing I knew, I'd signed a contract to sell them my pictures for a book on travel."

"That's incredible!" I darted a glance at Noah before turning my attention back to Rochester in time to stop him from eating a pile of cigarette butts. "How long did you spend travelling? Did you just do the one book or did you do more?"

"I took a year and managed one book of my own. Three other books included some of my work along with others. It was great to see so much of the world, but I always planned to come home. I'm not really a vagabond," he grinned. "I wanted stability and roots."

"I completely understand. That's why I came to Lake Claire too."

We walked on in companionable silence while Rochester nosed

around in mounds of leaves, sniffed garbage bags piled by the side of the road and tried to eat the roadside litter. We walked past the clearing in which I'd found the body the day before without stopping and continued on to the Jackson house. It looked as it always did; a sad shadow of a better time. I could easily envision it with a fresh coat of paint, ringing with the laughter of a large, happy family. The weather-beaten up wood siding and sagging porch seemed fitting, given its history.

"I love how tired and lived-in it looks, don't you? I think if I ever had the chance to fix it up, I'd still leave that weather-battered look. If everything was perfect, it would lose that feeling. Even if its past is a sad one, I'd still want to know it. That makes it real."

Noah studied the house intently.

"I think I agree. Even if someone did fix the place up, it wouldn't look right all neat and tidy. The neglect is kind of part of its charm."

I love that he understood. A tug on my arm had me looking around for Rochester, who'd taken advantage of my distraction to creep toward the porch and wedge himself underneath it, searching for more dog treasure.

"Rochester! Come here!"

I pulled at the leash as I walked toward the porch. I could see the wriggling hind end of my dog slowly emerging from under the steps.

"Nice move, dog," I said, exasperatedly. "Now I'm going to have to take the time to brush you and maybe even hose you down before I let you back in our clean apartment."

I had to chuckle as I reached down and tugged at Rochester's middle, pulling him out from under the porch. His pudgy stomach had gotten him stuck. My laughter died as I took in the object Rochester held firmly in his mouth. It was a finger bone.

"You have got to be kidding me."

My voice was the barest whisper, but Noah heard me and looked down at the dog.

"I guess this is going to be my newspaper's first exclusive."

I shot him a half-hearted glare and sank down on the soft grass, slipping one arm around Rochester as I dug in my pocket for my cell. Dialing 911, I brought it to my ear.

"911, please state the nature of your emergency."

I sighed and dropped my head against my knees as Noah sat down beside me.

"This is Wynne Forrester. I think I've just stumbled across a dead body – another one."

12

For the second day in a row, I stood on a gravel road outside of town and waited for the police to arrive. It seemed to take forever, but a glance at my watch showed only ten minutes had passed since Rochester had emerged from under the porch with his gruesome find. Noah pulled a small digital camera from his coat pocket and took a few shots of the house and porch before turning it toward me. I was busy fighting Rochester for the finger bone and only paused long enough to shoot Noah a quelling look before returning to my task. I finally persuaded Rochester to chew on a stick instead of the bone and tucked the finger inside a small plastic bag I kept in my pocket in case my dog decided to fertilize someone's lawn. A smile flitted across Noah's face at my expression.

"I'm glad you find my situation so amusing," I muttered. "You get a fantastic debut story for your paper, and I get to deal with annoyed policemen who probably think that I had something to do with these deaths since I keep finding the bodies. That's not exactly fair, you know."

The sound of sirens in the distance grew steadily louder and I could see the cloud of dust stirred up by the police car's advance.

"Unless I miss my guess, the cops are going to be more curious than annoyed, and no one could think you had anything to do with this after spending two minutes with you. Besides, curious busybodies will increase your sales. That's one bright spot in this whole mess. Another is that we have even more to go on for our investigation. A second skeleton this close to where you found the first one can't be a coincidence."

I rubbed Rochester's head before rising.

"You're right about that last bit–and probably about the busybodies too. Besides, this does give more credence to my theory that there was something very wrong about the way the Jacksons disappeared fifteen years ago. I need to figure out what really happened."

"We'll find out what happened and when we do, I'll print the truth of it. I wonder if God hasn't decided that it's time for everything that's been hidden to come to light. That's the best explanation I have for the fact that you've stumbled across two major clues in two days. There are no coincidences with God. I think when the truth finally comes out, you'll be vindicated in front of everyone who ever thought you were wrong, or worse, crazy."

"Speaking of which..." I nodded toward the road where a single police cruiser pulled into the Jackson drive and parked. The crime scene van was nowhere in sight, so I guessed that Sheriff Cynical–I meant Black–wanted to make certain I wasn't trying to extend my fame from the day before by faking a second victim.

My shoulders relaxed a bit when I saw that Sophie was the second figure emerging from the squad car.

"Miss Forrester," Sheriff Black nodded sharply in greeting. "What's this the dispatcher told me about you reporting another body?"

Yes, I thought, because it's my fault that someone got killed and buried under a porch. Finding a second set of remains was definitely not the way I'd envisioned my morning outing with Noah unfolding. I reigned in my temper.

"Actually," I said, "it was my dog this time. He was digging around under the porch and when I pulled him out, he had this finger bone clenched in his mouth."

I held up the baggie, passing it to Sheriff Black when he stretched out his hand for it. Sophie shot me a quick smile while the sheriff studied the finger bone and raised an eyebrow toward Noah. I felt myself blush, my reddened cheeks darkening further at the realization that Noah had caught her meaningful glance and was looking at me with a mischievous glint in his eyes. It was hard enough figuring out the whole man/woman thing one on one and now Sophie and Sheriff Black were trying to figure out our relationship. Fantastic.

"So, are you going to check under the porch to see what's there? Maybe, if there is a body under there, it's connected to the one I stumbled over in the clearing."

"Even if that were the case, Miss Forrester, it's none of your business, and nothing we can comment on."

I bristled at Sheriff Black's condescending tone.

"Maybe you would like it better if I believed that they belong to two individuals who died of natural causes within a mile of each other and buried themselves? Correct me if I'm wrong but I was under the impression that dead people aren't known for doing that."

Noah coughed, covering his smile with his hand. Sophie's face was impassive but her eyes were bright with amusement. It almost made up for the steely glare from Sheriff Black.

"Miss Forrester, please try to restrain yourself from using sarcasm. I don't think you want to antagonize me, do you?"

"Of course not, Sheriff, that's the last thing I want." I felt chagrined at my knee-jerk response. "I'm sorry. I just thought I'd point out a connection between the bodies is pretty logical."

"You should keep your comments confined to your witness statement. Sophie! Come over here and take Miss Forrester's statement. I'll call Mark and get crime scene out here and I'll take this gentleman's statement as soon as I'm done with that."

"It's Noah Sutton."

"What?"

"My name." Noah offered his hand and the sheriff shook it perfunctorily. "It's Noah Sutton."

"Fine. Mr. Sutton, just stay where you are until I can take your statement."

Noah nodded, unfazed by the sheriff's irritated tone. I envied his cool self-assurance. Sophie touched my arm and gestured that I follow her a few steps away so she could take my statement in private. I tugged on Rochester's leash and followed her to the edge of the driveway, about twenty-five feet away from where Noah and Sheriff Black stood next to the squad car. I glanced back at the house, expecting to feel a shiver of horror at the thought of a body buried beneath the front porch, but instead I just felt sad. I looked back at Sophie as she pulled out a notebook and pen. She flipped the book open, uncapped the pen and then met my eyes.

"All right, Wynne, I need you to tell me everything that happened from the time you arrived at the house until Sheriff Black and I arrived, including why you came out here this morning." She lowered her voice and leaned closer. "Once you've done that, you can tell me who the hot guy is and where you met him!"

I rolled my eyes, feeling myself blush despite my attempt to stay cool.

"You mean where you can find one like him, don't you?"

I chuckled at her unrepentantly enthusiastic nod, but my laugh caught in my throat as Sheriff Black shot me a dark look. Sophie caught the exchange and schooled her features into a mask of professionalism.

"Why don't you start by telling me what time you left your apartment this morning?"

"It was about six 'o clock when Noah picked me up, I think. We walked here at a pretty steady clip. It took maybe fifteen or twenty minutes."

In less time than it took to walk out to the Jackson place, I'd filled Sophie in on the details of our arrival at the house, Rochester's discovery and my subsequent call to 911. Sophie tucked her notebook into her jacket pocket just as the crime scene van showed up. The sheriff waved the CSI guys over, turning his back on Noah, who took advantage of the distraction to snap a few more pictures of the house and the crime scene techs.

"I'll see you later, Sophie. Will you let me know if you find anything out?"

I'd pitched my voice low but she still darted an apprehensive glance at the sheriff to be sure he hadn't heard me.

"If I can. Tell you what, let's meet for dinner tonight and catch up with each other. But before that, I'm going to need you both to come down to the station to sign your witness statements. I'm guessing you haven't signed yesterday's either, have you?"

She glanced significantly at Noah. She'd pump me for information mercilessly the minute she could. I knew it.

"I dropped by and signed the statement I gave yesterday while you were off shift. I can come by at my lunch break today, if that's okay. And yes, I'm up for dinner tonight. I don't know when Noah will have time to sign his statement. You'll have to ask him."

"Oh, I certainly will, my friend. If you hadn't found him first, I'd ask him all about his free time."

I tried to ignore the flare of jealousy I felt at her teasing words. Sophie was gorgeous, but she was also a loyal friend. She wasn't going to try to turn Noah's head. Anyway, the man didn't belong to me, so it's not like I could be upset if he did find her more attractive than me. No more drama. I thought fiercely, shoving down my insecurity. Seriously, Wynne. Grow up!

I said a quick goodbye to Sophie before tugging Rochester toward Noah. He turned with an easy grin, lifting his camera to snap a picture of my progress toward him. He had plenty of time to take it since Rochester had to examine every blade of grass we passed. I could feel my cheeks heating again and had to fight hard to crush my rising self-consciousness. I couldn't figure out if I was happy he wanted a picture of me or dreading the way I would look in it.

"Are you ready to go, or does the sheriff need you to stick around for a while?"

"I've been cleared to leave." He tucked the camera back into his jacket pocket. "Actually, I believe I'm about two seconds away from being ordered to leave. Shall we make our escape?"

I followed his gaze to where the sheriff was frowning in our direction. I wiggled the fingers of my free hand in a wave at the scowling man as we fell in step down the drive.

"You know, Noah," I said as we turned back toward town, "it seems like Sheriff Black is looking for a reason to be irritated with me. You'd think he thought I planned to drop a double-murder cold case in his lap. I hate it when people are upset with me, especially when it's something I can't fix."

"Come on," he reached over and took my hand, "let's go and get some breakfast. I don't know about you but I'm awfully hungry, even after what we found. We can sit for awhile, and I'll tell you all the reasons why this whole debacle is going to work out for good; starting with the fact that I met you."

I shivered in the cool morning air even as heat flushed my cheeks again. Glancing down at our clasped hands, I thought it looked to be a very good day – dead body and all.

13

_____

If I'd had any doubts about Noah's assertion that finding a body or two would make me a temporary town celebrity, they were gone within ten minutes of opening the store. Our breakfast had been great, but it was filled with interruptions from other diners. Everyone, as I was coming to expect in this town, had heard about the second body by the time we walked in the door to Trudy's. After breakfast, we'd parted ways outside my apartment with plans to make another trip to the Jackson house the following morning. Noah had smiled at me in a way I'd never been smiled at before. I was so taken off guard by it that I stammered my goodbye and smacked my head on my apartment door because I'd forgotten to open it. So much for my attempts at confident elegance, I thought with a wince.

I was happy to discover that stumbling over skeletons made for really good business. By noon, I'd made more sales than I had the entire previous week and all of the baked goods that

Martha had brought for the day were gone. I sent Jenny to beg for extra pastries while I kept ringing up sales and recounting the morning's events. Public interest was split evenly between my finding skeletons and my having breakfast with an eligible young man. In Lake Claire, dating was never just a two-person endeavor.

"So, Wynne," said Lisa, with a wide smile, "I hear you were sampling a pretty delicious dish at Trudy's this morning."

She laughed at my exaggerated groan. I glanced around for the kids, but I didn't see Oliver or Julia anywhere in the store. For once, I was glad not to see them. Little ears around during this kind of teasing often lead to embarrassing conversations at a later date.

"That's bad, even for you," I responded. "Usually you're a bit more subtle. And besides," I grinned, "I wasn't sampling; I was eyeing."

"I'm sure you were," she waggled her eyebrows, making me snort with laughter. "Okay, enough about that. I'll leave you alone...for now. If something does come of it, however, I'd better be the first to know."

"Naturally."

The bell above the door jingled and a gust of cool air rushed in along with three elderly women, breathless and rosy-cheeked, with knitted hats askew. I smiled at their haphazard apparel–coats buttoned wrong and slightly smeared lipstick–as I recognized my grandmother and her two closest friends. I privately thought they were Lake Claire's answer to the Spanish Inquisition.

There wasn't much gossip they didn't hear and they were merciless in ferreting it out. They might look cuddly and grandmotherly, but refuse to tell them something they wanted to know and you might as well have a tug of war with a pit-bull. There was about the same chance of either one releasing the bit.

"Oh, Wynne dear," my grandmother's bright blue eyes were filled with a mixture of concern and curiosity, "I could hardly believe my ears when Evelyn here told me that you and Noah, of all people, found a second body this morning! What on earth were you two doing out at the Jackson place so early anyway?"

"We were just going to check out the clearing where I found the skeleton yesterday but decided to go on and look at the Jackson house first. It's such an interesting place and a lovely walk."

"Really, Wynne," interrupted Evelyn Marshall in her no-nonsense tone, "I would have thought that you would have more sense than to wander around the countryside in the wee hours of the morning with a man. It doesn't look well for your reputation. Besides, Noah Sutton is hardly the kind of man you want to be seen with! The whole town is talking about you two."

I deliberately turned my back to grab the feather duster and took a moment to compose my features. Not because I was upset, but because I was afraid I'd laugh in her face and offend the poor woman. In a world of one night stands and relationships where casual sex was the norm, I'd hardly thought an early morning walk with a good-looking man would label me the town harlot. If it did, I might actually enjoy the temporary notoriety. I could actually envision these three ladies bearing down on me with a scarlet letter. I turned around and smiled at Mrs. Marshall.

"I suppose any man would have been an inappropriate companion for my early morning jaunt?" My inner imp danced with glee as I unashamedly turned it loose on poor Mrs. Marshall, dusting the counter vigorously as I spoke. "After all, anyone could have seen us out there, on a public road, in full view of town. Rest assured that next time I'll be certain to find a secluded spot for our visit so that no one will see us together. We could plan to arrive separately, from different directions even, and speak in whispers the whole time. Of course," I mused, "we'll have to stand quite close to hear each other. That could present a problem."

There was an odd sound coming from Lisa's direction and I knew she was trying to cover her laughter. My grandmother and her two friends stared at me with such identical expressions of horror that I couldn't keep a straight face. I laughed and slipped out from behind the counter to put a friendly arm around Mrs. Marshall.

"I'm sorry, Mrs. Marshall, that was quite wicked of me!" I tried to look apologetic, still giggling. "I've no intention of meeting Noah Sutton or any other man in secluded areas for any reason, romantic or otherwise."

"Well!" huffed Mrs. Marshall indignantly. "I should hope not; and you'd do well to watch your tongue, young lady!"

"I know it," I responded cheerfully, "but I felt sure your excellent sense of humor would enable you to forgive me, just this once."

A reluctant smile tugged at the older woman's lips as Grandma put a warm arm around my waist.

"My granddaughter is a spitfire, ladies, and she comes by it honestly. I'm sure that you can remember more than one occasion when my tongue got me into trouble. Besides that, Evelyn, you're one to talk–or, don't you remember what you said to Patty Burns when she cornered you outside the schoolhouse and yelled at you for refusing to go to the senior class picnic with her brother?"

Evelyn turned beet red. I was worried she was going to erupt in anger, but then she started laughing so hard that she had to sit down on one of the stools I kept by the counter before her legs gave out. I grabbed a bottle of water and set it in front of her, watching in fascination as she sipped it between bouts of giggles. My grandmother's eyes were full of fun as she turned to me.

"You have to understand, Wynne. Evelyn would never have said what she did to anyone, but Patty Burns. That woman, even at seventeen, was a bitter, sharp-tongued harpy, and she never grew out of it. She was miserable her whole life. No matter how kind we tried to be, she never could be anything but mean."

"What did you say, Mrs. Marshall?" asked Lisa, tapping her foot impatiently. "Please, tell us."

"Oh, well, I said that I thought she would want to thank me for turning down the only escort she was likely to get–unless she walked her dog to the class picnic."

It was so quiet you could have heard a pin drop. Evelyn looked around sheepishly.

"What? I couldn't very well let him take me there when Rosie was sweet on him and Patty was horrible!"

"Evelyn!" My grandmother's horrified expression was highlighted by her reddened cheeks. "That was a secret!"

"Oh, Rosie, come now," piped up Doris Mayberry, laying a comforting hand on my grandmother's arm, "the whole thing happened over sixty years ago, and everyone knew Donald Burns was a flirt. He's also been dead for forty years. Those are good reasons to get over your embarrassment. Buy a book from your granddaughter so we can make it back to your place in time for Jeopardy. I've got three dollars that say I'm going to win Final Jeopardy this time. You two don't stand a chance."

Grandma and her friends each picked up a novel, paid, gave me baby-powder scented hugs and went out into the darkening late afternoon just as Sophie walked in. I glanced up from the till with a welcoming smile and waved as Lisa slipped out the door.

"Hey Sophie," I walked around the counter and gave her a quick hug, "how was the rest of the fight for law and order today?"

"Well, nobody else has turned up a dead body, so I'm afraid town gossip will be fixed on you for the foreseeable future."

"That's not true!" I protested. "I heard that the entire fifth grade class at Lake Claire Elementary was in tears today because Mr. Chubbs was found toes up in the classroom after morning recess."

"Mr. Chubbs was a hamster, Wynne."

Sophie's look was long-suffering. I shrugged.

"Well, if you're going to be picky about it..."

I managed to look down my nose at her, but snickered when I caught a glimpse of my reflection in the store window. The darkening sky outside combined with the lights inside had turned the windows into mirrors.

"You're a very strange woman, Wynne. You know that, right?"

"The fact was never in doubt, my friend. Listen. Why don't you give me a half hour to finish up here for the night? We can meet up at the restaurant for supper, if that's easiest."

"Would you mind if we just picked something up and ate at your place, Wynne? After two days of watching the CSI guys exhume skeletons and handing out parking tickets because my boss is in a foul temper, I could use some girl time."

"That sounds perfect to me. What do you want, Chinese or pizza? I can call it in now, and it'll be ready by the time I'm finished here."

"Chinese sounds great. I'll stop in at the Shangri-La and pick it up once I've changed out of my uniform. Can you order me some extra hot and sour soup?"

"I don't know how you can stand that stuff, but I'll order it if you promise to keep your fingers off my ginger beef."

"You'd better order extra of both," replied Sophie as she opened the door. "Last time I thought you were going to scratch my eyes out over the last chicken ball."

I waved her away, picking up the phone to place the order.

"Food is serious business for some of us. I'll get extra of everything so that both we and our friendship survive the evening."

Her laugh chimed with the bell above the door, lingering in the air as she left. I placed the order for supper and then did a final walkthrough, picking up and re-shelving stray books in their proper sections. I hummed to myself as I grabbed the broom to do a quick tidy of the floor, laughing when I realized I was humming "Food, Glorious Food" from the musical Oliver!

"Nice choice, Wynne," I murmured, swinging the broom to and fro, "and for my next number, "Diamonds are a Girl's Best Friend."

I did a little sashay and wiggled my hips in my very best Marilyn Monroe imitation, giggling all the while. I was have so much fun belting out the show tune that I missed to sound of the bells above the door ringing until I came face to face with Noah, red-faced and shaking with suppressed laughter of his own.

"Right," I cleared my throat as my face suffused with the warmth of embarrassment, "note to self. Lock store before indulging secret dreams of Broadway."

Noah wiped his eyes with the backs of his hands as his chuckling slowed.

"I don't know; I would have been sad to miss that performance."

"I didn't realize I was giving one," I muttered, feeling the tips of my ears burn.

"That's what made it so entertaining. The only times I've seen you, you've been so calm and peaceful. Even your sense of humour is subtle. I like that side of you a lot, but I think I like this side of you just as much."

"As nice as that is to hear, I'd feel a lot more comfortable if you'd even the score and do a number of your own."

He grinned and shook his head.

"No way, lady. On you it's cute, but if I tried a song and dance number, you'd laugh me out of your store and never want to see me again."

"That's highly unlikely, but I'll give you a pass...for now. Just know that I'm going to be watching to see if I can catch you doing something equally idiotic. Everyone's got at least one quirk of some kind, and I'll figure yours out yet."

"I suppose that's only fair. Just don't expect me to make it easy for you."

"It wouldn't be any fun if you made it easy. You're just lucky that I've got my mind on the two skeletons that have been recovered or you wouldn't stand a chance of keeping me from finding it out."

"I don't doubt it. Anyway, I just dropped by to hand deliver the first edition of the *Lake Claire Times*. You made the front page. Well, sort of."

My gaze dropped to the paper he held out, and I burst out laughing. Rochester's somber face looked up at me. The tip of my foot was just visible in the left hand corner of the picture. "It's official, then. My left foot is about to become famous. Should I insure it like Betty Grable did her legs?"

"That would be a wise decision," Noah's lips twitched, "since I've been known to step on toes once or twice in my lifetime and we are still going to walk together tomorrow morning. I hope Rochester will still deign to associate with us now that he's such an important figure."

I swatted his arm with the folded paper. "Ha, ha. Sorry to kick you out, but I need to close the shop so I can have supper with Sophie. Don't worry, though. I'll remind Rochester that it's never a good idea to offend your photographer. They can easily exact revenge, and do it publicly."

"Alright, alright, I'm going. I'll meet you tomorrow morning at 6:30. Maybe Sophie will be able to tell you something about the investigation–though I doubt she's supposed to."

"That's what I'm hoping. It may be a guessing game, but she and I have enough trust built up that she'll let me know what she can. I'll leave alone what she can't talk about."

"I'll see you later, then...Marilyn."

"Brat!"

He was grinning widely as he ran for the door, stopping just long enough to hold it open for Jenny. She sent me a curious look but didn't comment on my flustered expression as she helped me finish tidying up the store.

"I'm going to take off now, Jenny. Can you lock up? I want to get Rochester fed and watered before Sophie gets to my place with dinner."

"I'm good here; you go on ahead and take care of our local celebrity."

She smiled and nodded at the paper in my hand. I shook my head.

"There'll be no living with Rochester once he sees this–at least

97

not for a few days. Then someone else will be front-page news and people will have to stop spoiling him."

Jenny arched a brow at me and took the broom my hands.

"You do know he's just a dog, right? He can't read."

"Good point. That does make things considerably easier."

I waved goodbye as she started to sweep, pulling my coat from the rack behind the counter and slipping it on as I pushed the door open. I stuck a hand in my coat pocket and pulled my keys out, humming again as I moved swiftly around the building to the back stairs. I'd just set my foot on the bottom stair when a shiver ran down my spine, and I turned around to look behind me. Nothing. There was no one behind me. In fact, no one anywhere on the street. I looked both ways, up and down, but I couldn't see anything out of the ordinary. Rolling my shoulders, I started up the staircase still unable to shake the feeling I was being watched.

I breathed a sigh of relief as I reached the landing, stretching my hand out to fit my keys into the lock by feel since I kept forgetting to put up an outdoor light. A light brush on the top of my hand had me stifling a scream, and I took an involuntary half-step back. Hanging from the doorframe was a shadowy shape I hadn't noticed earlier. It was too dark to see any details, but I could tell that it had the shape of a miniature person. I quickly unlocked my door and reached in to flick on the lights. I felt the blood drain from my face as my eyes adjusted to take in the doll with a noose around her neck, hanging from a nail driven into the frame. With trembling fingers, I carefully opened the small white note pinned to her shirt.

You're next.

14

"I can't believe you called the sheriff over something this childish, Sophie." I moved to pick up the doll from my kitchen table, but she grabbed my arm to stop my progress. "Oh, come on, I was going to be careful. I just wanted to take a closer look."

"Stop whining and keep your hands to yourself. If I hadn't seen you reaching for the doll when I was walking toward your steps with our supper, your fingerprints would be on it. They're already on the note, and the sheriff will be less likely to take this seriously if he finds your prints on everything."

I sighed and crossed my arms, rubbing my hands over them to try to warm myself up. Rochester nudged my knee with his nose, aware that I was upset.

"He won't take it seriously anyway–even though that doll looks an awful lot like me."

"It does," agreed Sophie, reaching down to pet Rochester's head, "right down to a tiny little smirk on its mouth."

"Nice. Thanks for that. Maybe we should eat our take-out before it gets any colder. I need to tell you how I embarrassed myself in front of Noah so you can laugh at me–preferably before the sheriff gets here. I don't mind telling you, but Sheriff Black would consider it a confirmation that I'm a total idiot."

"He comes across pretty harsh, but the sheriff is actually slightly more objective than you'd think–slightly. So, tell me what happened with Noah. I'm glad you said I could laugh, because there's no way I'm holding it in."

"I'd be disappointed if you didn't. A story like this one deserves some serious mocking. Just wait until I tell you what he caught me doing."

She was still chuckling, wiping tears of laughter from her cheeks, when a knock sounded at the door, announcing the sheriff's arrival. I opened it slowly to give her a minute to compose herself before facing her boss. He was here to talk to me, but she'd still want him to see her as professional. I couldn't blame her for that. I gestured Sheriff Black in.

"The note and the doll are on the table, Sheriff," I said. "I touched the note when I read it, but Sophie kept me from handling the doll. She used gloves when she took it down and she took pictures first to show you how it was hanging."

He glanced over at Sophie, his expression unreadable.

"Why didn't you leave it as it was, Sophie? You had to know I would want to see that."

"I know, sir, but it's pretty windy out and I was worried that if there were any fibers or DNA, the breeze would affect that. I thought it more prudent to take pictures and then remove it and put it somewhere safer. I made the call I thought was best."

"Fine." His tone was curt as he turned to me. "Miss Forrester, can you explain to me why someone would leave you a death threat?"

I stared at him. "I'm pretty sure I haven't done anything deserving of it, if that's what you're insinuating, Sheriff." I knew my irritation was clear. "I found two bodies, so maybe their killer is worried that I know something about their deaths? I don't know. Other than that, the only reason someone has to be angry with me is if they think I charged them too much for the latest bestseller."

"Your sarcasm isn't helping your situation. I thought I warned you about that this morning."

"Well, your obvious prejudice isn't helping it either!" I took a deep breath, seeing the warning in Sophie's gaze. "Listen, I know you're just trying to do your job, Sheriff. I'm not trying to make it more difficult. I've had the misfortune, however, of stumbling onto things I would rather not have seen and you're acting like I planned it!"

"Did you?"

I threw up my hands in frustration. "No! I hope if I ever did kill someone, I'd be smarter about it than putting myself in your crosshairs by finding the body myself. I didn't plan anything. I went for a walk; found a body. I went for another walk; found another body. I'm going for another walk tomorrow, and I'm really hoping that these things don't come in threes."

He watched me silently for a minute before he shifted his gaze to the table. Walking over, he studied the doll and note lying in the center, far from the reaches of Rochester's eager mouth. He set down the case I hadn't even noticed he was carrying and opened it, pulling out two evidence bags and a pair of tweezers. Without a word, he used them to place the doll in one bag and the note in another, sealing them both carefully before tucking them into the case and closing it.

"Do you have any more questions, Sheriff?" I hoped that my voice sounded politer than I felt. "I'd be happy to answer anything you feel is relevant."

"Not at this time. I'll be sure to let you know if we find anything out about this, but I wouldn't get your hopes up. The odds of finding fingerprints or DNA are slim, and since it's not a priority, the lab won't get to it anytime soon. We do have two skeletons that we're dealing with at the moment, you know."

I ignored his sarcasm, biting my tongue to keep a comment about it being okay for him but not for me from spilling out. I gestured him ahead of me to the door. I'd already made things worse for myself by losing my temper; I needed to watch my step if I didn't want to end up any higher on the Sheriff's list of suspects. Sophie stayed back and started setting out our dinner. "Good evening, Sheriff. I hope it's quiet from here on out."

"'Night, Miss Forrester; I'll let you know if and when I have any information for you."

"I appreciate it. Thank you."

I shut the door behind him and turned to Sophie, my face already showing my chagrin.

"I know," I held up a hand, "I should have controlled my temper better than I did. But does he seriously think I had anything to do with those bodies other than finding them? Come on!"

"He's being thorough, Wynne," she said as she opened the take-out containers, "and that's a good thing. The sooner he eliminates you as a suspect, the sooner he'll actually start looking into who hung that doll from your door. Until then, please, will you watch your step?"

I sighed. "Of course I will. It probably doesn't mean anything but I have to admit, I'm a bit frightened that someone would make a death threat toward me. Even if it's fake."

"You don't know it's fake." Her expression was serious. "Maybe it is, but maybe it's not. Like I said, you need to watch yourself."

"Okay–okay, I promise, I will. Now, can we eat already? I'm starving."

After another moment, she smiled and the tension seeped from the air.

"You bet–but who's picking the movie? If you want one of those old musicals, I won't fight you, but, honestly, I'd rather watch something with lots of action and explosions."

"You're such a cop."

"I know."

The music was just starting for the first worship song when I walked through the doors of Lake Claire Community Church on Sunday morning. I hate running late, but I just seem to move slower on Sundays. Still, I wasn't really late; more like right on time. I hurried into the sanctuary and looked around for an open spot in the pews. To my surprise, Noah was sitting by the aisle in a pew a few steps ahead of me. As if sensing my eyes on him, he turned around. He smiled when he spotted me and waved me forward, patting the spot next to him as he slid over.

"Hi," I whispered, tucking my purse under the pew, "It's good to see you here."

"I thought it was about time," he whispered back.

He was about to speak again when the worship leader told everyone to rise, and we started singing. I lost myself in the music, eyes closing as I breathed deep and opened my heart to God. This was one of my favorite parts of Sunday mornings. The worship team finished the last song and put away their instruments while Josh walked out on the stage. I sat down and pulled my Bible out of my purse. I glanced over and saw Noah picking up a weathered Bible from next to him, wondering idly if it was the same one the Anglican priest had given him.

"I should probably get a new Bible sometime, "he whispered, as though he'd read my thoughts, "but this one has so much sentimental meaning. Besides, it falls open to all my favorite passages and when I read them, I remember how God has spoken to me in the past."

"I love that."

This morning's sermon was on taming the tongue from James 3, and it had me confessing the way I'd let my words get away from me lately. I started to wonder if the rest of the congregation were feeling equally convicted, since I'd been such a topic of gossip the past few weeks, but a gentle nudge in my heart told me it wasn't my business. I was supposed to be concerned with my own response to God; not to try to do his job in other people. It was a constant battle for me to remember that he worked as He saw fit, not as I did.

"So, what do you usually do for lunch after church?" Noah asked as we stood to sing a final song.

"I don't really have set plans. Sometimes I meet Josh and Lisa and their kids at Trudy's and sometimes I just go home. I was thinking of seeing if they're free today. Do you want to come with us?"

"Sure, if you don't mind me crashing your party. I'd like to get to know them. That sermon hit me right where it hurts. I really needed that."

I smiled at him and felt my heart warm toward him even more. The more I got to know of Noah, the clearer his character became–and the more I liked him. What his latest comment revealed was the most attractive thing I'd encountered yet, and I was already feeling awfully attracted.

Noah stuck by my side as I wound my way through the foyer toward Lisa. The gleam in her eye when she spotted us together told me she'd have some questions later but, to her credit, she was nothing but friendly. She said that they were free for lunch and quickly seconded my invitation to Noah.

"I just need to get the kids from the nursery and Josh will be free in not too long. Want to meet at Trudy's in about a half hour?"

"Sure. I think I'll run home and change and then meet you there. Does that work for you, Noah?"

"Perfect. I think I'll do the same."

After visiting with a few more people, Noah and I finally made it outside. I'd walked to church so I started down the sidewalk toward my apartment.

"Do you mind if I walk with you?" he asked. "My place is just a five minute walk from yours, and yours is right on the way."

"That'd be nice. Thanks."

We didn't talk as we walked down the street toward my apartment, but it was a comfortable silence. In less than ten minutes, he'd seen me to my door and was making his way further down Main Street. I watched him for a minute before unlocking my door and entering my apartment. Rochester's head lifted and he studied me with wise brown eyes from his place near the sofa in the living room. I walked over and laid a hand on his head, rubbing his ears gently.

"Rochester, I think I'm in deep trouble here. I'm having lunch with Noah and the Taylors, and I'm a bit afraid of what will happen if Lisa gets it into her head that he's interested in me. Or," I qualified, "if she tells him flat out that I'm definitely attracted to him. I could see her doing it too."

The dog just rolled over onto his back, waiting for me to scratch his belly.

"Obviously, you're really concerned for my peace of mind, Rochester. Thank you for that." I sighed. "Okay. I'm an adult. I can do this. And, it's true, right? I really, really like that man."

My stomach clenched as I spoke the words out loud. It was nerve-wracking, but for the first time in my life, I was ready to take the risk to see where a relationship would lead. With a whispered prayer for courage and wisdom, I got up and headed for my bedroom. I had clothes to change if I wanted to make it to Trudy's on time and, if Noah was going to be there, I definitely didn't want to be late.

15

"Wynne! Did you hear? The police know who the bones you found belong to!"

I swung around, dropping from the books I was shelving.

"Dot? What are you doing here? Aren't you supposed to be working right now? I thought you always took the day shift."

Dot closed the door behind her and stomped her foot impatiently. She was still wearing her uniform from Trudy's but she'd tossed her coat on over it, not bothering to button it in her hurry.

"It doesn't matter if I'm supposed to be working or not, Wynne. I told Frank that I needed a few minutes to run over here and tell you the latest news. Have you heard it yet, or did I beat everyone else?"

I smiled at her eagerness. Sophie had told me that the police had some leads, but that was all I'd heard until now. My heart sped up at the thought of finding out who had been buried in the grove or under the porch of the Jackson place. I wondered which body had been identified.

"No, I haven't heard that, Dot. You're the first to bring the news. Now, tell me everything. Which set of remains was identified?"

"Well, it turns out," she said, settling on a stool in front of the coffee counter, "that the bones from the body under the porch belong to Mrs. Jackson."

"Are you sure? Did they do DNA testing or something?"

I could hardly believe it. If that body belonged to Mrs. Jackson, I was right that their disappearance was part of a crime. I came over to the far side of the coffee counter, poured Dot a cup and grabbed a scone, setting both in front of her. She picked up the scone and bit in, speaking around the mouthful of pastry.

"They ran the DNA against the toothbrushes–or hairbrushes, I can't remember which–they still had in evidence from when the family disappeared fifteen years ago. It's conclusive. Deputy Mason was talking about it at the restaurant, and I just had to come over and tell you." She sipped her coffee and sighed. "I have to say, it's nice to be off my feet in the middle of the day for a change."

"You deserve more breaks than you get, Dot. You should tell Frank I said so. But, back to what you were saying. Do they know who the second set of bones belongs to yet? Do they know how Mrs. Jackson died? Was she murdered?"

"I don't know much else, Wynne. The second body is still unidentified, I think, but Deputy Mason did say that Mrs. Jackson died under suspicious circumstances."

"Well, obviously, since her whole family disappeared!"

"I know!" She shook her head and lowered her voice, even

though there was no one else in the shop with us. "I think he just doesn't want to admit the fact she was murdered. When I pressed him, he added that the cause of death wasn't natural, but he wouldn't say anything else."

"That's more information than I had, so I'll take it." I leaned my elbows on the counter. "Thanks for coming by to tell me. I know the police aren't happy that Noah and I have been hunting down information, and that he's been printing what we've found. They might be upset with you for telling me anything."

Dot shrugged and hopped off the stool, moving with the energy of a woman twenty years her junior.

"I'm not too worried. What are they going to do? If they try anything with me, Frank will refuse to feed them and then where will they be? Deputy Mason eats at Trudy's almost every day, and the Sheriff's in a few times a week. I happen to know that Sophie's on your side, so I'm covered."

"Thanks again," I slipped an arm around her shoulders and squeezed gently. "You're a good friend, Dot."

She hugged me back and then headed toward the door.

"You've been good for the town, Wynne. Your grandparents are happy to have you here and it's so nice having a bookstore here instead of having to drive into the city or order online to get what I want. Besides, you're a sweet girl. It's been fun watching Noah try to get your attention."

I blushed, feeling my ears burn. Noah and I weren't exactly dating, but we weren't exactly only friends. In the three months since we'd found the second body, we'd been spending a lot of time together, and I was going crazy trying to figure out how he felt about me. Crazy–but not quite enough to outright ask the man if he saw me as more than a friend. Soon, I promised myself, I would ask soon. I couldn't take much more of my heart fluttering every time I saw him without knowing if we were headed for something serious.

"I don't know that he's trying all that hard," I murmured finally.

"Oh, he is. You trust me, my girl. I know men, and he's got his eye on you. Just you wait. He'll make a move soon, I'm sure."

I smiled weakly, waving as she shut the door behind her. I'd just have to wait to see if she was right, but it was nice that she thought Noah was interested. It was flattering, since I still couldn't quite believe that someone would be attracted to me. I figured that even if a guy liked what he saw, the more he got to know me, the more he'd realize that I was too much work for too little payoff. Cynical, yes, but that was how I felt. Recognizing the beginning stirrings of self-pity, I shook my head and forced myself to focus on the work at hand.

I'd only been back at the bookshelves, reorganizing things, for ten minutes when the doorbell jingled, and I turned around to see the man in question walking through the door. Noah glanced around, smile widening when he saw that the shop was empty.

"Hey – did you hear the latest news?"

His greeting so closely echoed Dot's that I laughed.

"Dot was just here to tell me that they've identified the body from under the porch. Mrs. Jackson; can you believe it, Noah? We were right."

"I know. And," he moved closer, face alight with intensity, "I have more information than that."

I stepped away from the bookshelves and hurried over. "What is it? What did you find out?"

"They found arsenic," his voice lowered, "trace amounts of it still present in the bones. It means that she was being poisoned slowly over a long period of time. Now who do you think would have enough access to her food and drink to do that?"

"My immediate response is her husband or kids," I paused, thinking, "but the Children of the Elements spent a lot of time together. It could have been any of them, couldn't it?"

"Maybe. But it gets better."

"What do you mean?"

"It wasn't the arsenic that killed her."

My mouth dropped open and I stared at him. "What did you say?"

"I said it wasn't the arsenic that killed her. She was being poisoning steadily, and would likely have died from it within months, but her death was caused by strangulation. Her hyoid bone was broken clean through."

"Strangulation? Oh, what a horrible way to die!"

"I know."

"Wait a minute," I said as a thought struck. "If she was strangled, the odds are higher that she knew her killer, aren't they? I mean, he'd have to get close enough to touch, right?"

"It makes sense, but I wouldn't want to make any assumptions yet. We still need more evidence."

"What are the police planning to do?"

Noah shrugged. "Officially reopen the case, I suppose. I'm sure we'll find out soon enough."

"Right. But this new information makes me want to figure out the mystery even more."

"Me, too," he reached out and took hold of my hand. "Listen, Wynne, this is probably the worst timing ever, but I've wanted to ask you something for quite awhile and I wasn't sure how."

My heart sped up and I tried not to look as nervous as I felt. "What is it, Noah? You can ask me anything, you know that."

Did that make me sound overeager. Desperate? I hoped not.

"You must know by now how much I like spending time with you," he began, and my stomach clenched. Was he preparing me for the "just friends" talk?

"I like spending time with you too."

"Well, I was hoping that you like it enough to maybe..." his voice trailed off. I waited, holding my breath.

"Maybe what, Noah?"

"Maybe...maybe, consider being my girlfriend? I feel like I'm too old to call you my girlfriend, but I'm not sure what other word to use."

My heart was beating like mad by now I had to ask some questions before I totally lost my ability to think.

"What do you mean by "girlfriend"? If you mean someone to be your significant other without much thought for the future, that's one thing. If you mean," I forced myself not to flinch as I looked him in the face, "the woman that you're thinking might be the one you marry, that's different. Which do you mean?" I prayed that I hadn't just ruined everything, but I had to know.

"I mean," he said, eyes meeting mine squarely, "the woman that I'm thinking might be the one I want to marry. I think we need more time together to find that out, but I really, really like what I've seen so far."

"You're sure?" I knew I sounded skeptical. I'd never been this close to a serious commitment before, and, as much as I wanted it, it seemed too good to be true.

"I'm sure, Wynne. I've never met anyone like you, and I want to know that we're both on the same page. I want to grow closer to you and see where God leads us. I've been praying about it and I feel peace about looking toward a future together. I just need to know if that's something you're interested in."

I closed my eyes and took a deep breath. *God, this is such a huge gift from you. If it's right, will you show us? If not, then I'm asking you to make that clear too.*

"I'm very interested, Noah. A bit terrified, but definitely interested."

"Okay. Good. Really?"

I laughed at the look on his face. It was a mix of hope, conviction and uncertainty. I had a sneaking suspicion it was the mirror image of my own expression. "Really."

He pulled me a bit closer, his thumb rubbing the back of my hand. "I have another question, Wynne."

"What's that?" I sounded breathless.

"Can I kiss you to seal the agreement?"

"Oh," I could feel myself start to smile, "I think that could be arranged."

His face lowered toward mine and my eyes slid shut. Just before his lips touched mine, I gasped, and he jerked his head up in surprise.

"What is it?"

"I just realized that I didn't tell you. I've never done this before! What if I'm horrible at it?"

I could feel sweat breaking out on my forehead as my nerves took over. He grinned and lowered his head again until his lips were almost on mine.

"You won't be, but even if you are, we'll just have to practice."

He was right; I wasn't. But we practiced anyway.

16

I wondered if dating Noah would affect our investigation, but it turned that I needn't have worried about it. We didn't really "date" so much as spend time together the way we had been–with a few romantic surprises thrown in for good measure. After two months, I was getting more used to the delight of receiving flowers and other little gifts. It turned out that my–well, my gentleman caller was how I referred to him, much to everyone's amusement–was quite a romantic. The chances of my heart getting away from him were slim to none, and I didn't want to take it back anyway. Noah was everything I'd ever dreamt of; godly and hard-working but not critical of others. He could be impatient sometimes, and a bit too task-focused when he was busy, but I certainly had flaws too.

"You're thinking about Noah again," said Jenny smugly.

I blushed and started, realizing I'd been leaning on the broom I was using to sweep the café section of the bookstore and daydreaming. I picked it up and started sweeping again, smiling at Jenny as she walked past with an armload of books. We were due to open in five minutes, so I was glad she'd called me back to reality.

"I can't seem to help myself, Jenny. It's a bit maddening, actually. I feel like I'm fifteen, mooning over my first crush instead of nearly thirty and trying to have an adult relationship."

"Well, I think it's cute," she said over her shoulder as she started shelving books. "You guys are so well-suited. You do know that we're all taking bets as to when he's going to pop the question, right?"

My stomach clenched, and I could feel myself pale.

"Let's not go there just yet, okay? I'm just getting used to this whole dating thing. I think we both need some time before we're ready to plan a wedding. For now, we're focusing on getting to know each other as best friends."

"Best friends who just happen to kiss each other," she laughed.

"The best kind of best friends," I said, smug in my own right, "and we're careful not to spend too much time kissing. We want to keep it special and be sure we're honoring God."

"I have to respect your restraint. My husband and I were so young when we started dating and got married. We made it to the wedding as virgins, but just barely. It's a difficult commitment, but worth it. Our first years of marriage were rocky enough without the added guilt of having slept together beforehand."

"I've seen enough friends walk through some really rough times after giving in that I want to be doubly sure I'm wise in romance. We've been praying together and separately, and it seems like God is leading us together but we both said we're open to whatever He has for the future–together or apart. It's scary," I admitted," but I know what it's like when I don't surrender my plans to God. That's a bad idea all the way around."

"You said it."

I walked to the storage closet and put the broom away before heading to unlock the door. Outside, I could see the other merchants on Main Street getting ready to open. I loved the sense of community; the feeling that I really belonged. The shop was doing good business. It didn't make a huge profit, but it did well enough for me to live comfortably and that was really all I wanted. If Noah and I did end up marrying sometime in the future, the fact that we both wanted roots in Lake Claire would make things go that much more smoothly. I glanced out the window as I flipped the sign from "Closed" to "Open" and spotted Noah walking down the street toward the shop, as if I'd conjured him just by thinking about him.

I could smell the coffee perking and I'd set the scones and muffins on display under glass covers. With everything ready to go, I moved toward the front of the store just as the door opened and Noah walked through. I walked over to greet him, smiling as he leaned down to drop a kiss on my cheek.

"Hey," he said, slipping an arm around my waist. "How's business?"

"I don't know. We just opened two minutes ago, and you're our first customer."

"I'll have to make it worth your while, then. Are we still on for dinner tonight?"

"I'm planning on it. Trudy's, take-out, or do you want to make something together?"

"I have some steaks in the fridge. Why don't you come over after work, and I'll throw them on the grill. It won't be as good as barbecuing them, but with this weather," he gestured outside at the snow-covered streets that marked the advent of Christmas, "I don't want to be standing on my deck to cook."

"I don't blame you. I do love the snow, though."

"Yeah, I know you do," he shot me a wry grin, "a fact I discovered when you challenged me to a snowball fight last Saturday."

"It's not my fault you can't hit the broadside of a barn," I teased.

"You can't either, but you're not above dirty tactics. A handful of snow down the jacket is not pleasant – or fair."

"I wouldn't have had to do that if you hadn't dropped a pile of the stuff on my head; so there."

"We should probably stay inside tonight if we don't want to end up in an all-out brawl in the snow."

"Agreed," I leaned into his arm and smiled up at him. "So, do you have anything new to tell me about the police investigation? Sophie's been keeping me up to date, but even she doesn't have much these days. Do you think they'll ever figure out who that second skeleton is?"

"I hope so, but it's not looking great. I did have an idea, though. That's actually why I dropped by."

"Do tell," I lowered my voice even though Jenny was still at the back of the store, shelving things. "What are you thinking?"

"I was doing a little more research on the Children of the Elements and I had a brainwave. I thought I'd do a search for similar groups in this area, and if I didn't find anything, expand the search countrywide. As it happens, I hit on something in the next county."

I could feel my excitement growing. This was the first real lead we'd had in months. The police were stymied, though they weren't admitting it. It was obvious, though, that they had nothing to go on. If we could gather more information, it might help them finally identify the second victim. All they did know was that the second victim was strangled too; that news had come out a month ago.

"What kind of group? Where exactly are they? Who are the leaders?"

Noah held up his hands at my rapid-fire delivery.

"I don't know much yet," he said, "but I'm planning a trip over to Hastings to find out. That's where they're located."

"I'm coming with you."

"I don't know if that's a great idea, Wynne."

"I'm coming with you," I repeated, daring him to argue.

"Okay, you're coming with me." Concern lit his gaze. "I just worry about your safety, you know? It's not that I don't think you can do this."

"I know," I squeezed his hand, "and I'm sorry if I get a bit militant about the independent woman thing. But I do want to come with you."

"How about we go tonight, then? We can grab dinner in Hastings and look around a bit, see what we can find out, if you're willing to postpone our quiet steak dinner at home."

"Done," I grinned, bouncing on my toes. "Pick me up after work? I'll get Sophie or Jenny to check on Rochester."

"Sure; now I really need to get to work. The paper doesn't write itself."

"Have a good day, okay?"

After a quick kiss goodbye, he left and headed toward his office. Jenny was still discreetly shelving books at the back of the store, so I headed for the front counter just as the bell signalled the arrival of more customers. Turning to greet them, I focused on the day ahead, praying it would pass quickly. The prospect of answers to the mystery that had been looming for so long was addictive and I was in need of a fix.

Hastings was only twenty miles from Lake Claire, but we took it slow in deference to the winter roads. After a half hour, Noah and I pulled up in front of a small diner that looked remarkably similar to Trudy's. Every small town I'd been to had one; the favourite meeting place and hub of local gossip. I was hoping that they had a waitress as chatty as Dot and that she'd be willing to talk with us. Noah held the door open for me and followed me inside. I spotted an empty booth and headed toward it, sliding onto the worn vinyl while slipping my coat and scarf off.

"Do you want coffee or something else to start?"

I looked up to see a pretty, pleasantly rounded woman in her forties standing next to our table with a coffeepot in hand.

"Just water for me, I think," I said, glancing at Noah.

"Water's good," he replied. "What do you recommend for dinner?"

The woman, whose name tag identified her as Laura, propped a hand on her hip.

"The meatloaf is good and so are the burgers. I wouldn't go for fish–it's never fresh–but the cook does a good job with grilled chicken."

"Grilled chicken sounds great to me," I said, smiling. "Can I get a baked potato with that and a tossed salad?"

"Sure. And for you?" She switched her gaze to Noah.

"I'll have the meatloaf with mashed potatoes and whatever cooked vegetables you have as a side. Thanks."

"No problem."

She walked over to the kitchen to place our orders, returning quickly with two large glasses of ice water. She set them down in front of us and started to walk away, but Noah stopped her.

"Laura, do you have a minute to tell us about the town? We're from Lake Claire, and we thought we'd drive over to check out the alternative remedies store. A friend of mine said that they sell healing crystals and my girlfriend," he gestured to me, "has some health trouble that the doctors can't seem to help her with. Besides," he winked conspiratorially at the waitress, "it gets me in her good books when I buy her pretty stuff."

Laura smiled, but her eyes were guarded. "You picked the right day to come," she said, "because Inner Pieces is open late on Thursdays and Fridays. The shop owner is," she paused, "interested in teaching people about his way of life. He can be pretty intense, though."

"Intense?" I met Noah's gaze and pretended concern. "I don't know if I want to feel forced into something I'm not comfortable with. I just thought I'd give those crystals a try if they looked nice. I don't want to end up involved in some weird religion or something. He's not into that, Laura, is he?"

"He's pretty convinced that his way is the right way," she said. "Listen, I probably shouldn't be telling you this. Mitchell has some powerful friends in town, and they think his business is good for us. Personally, the guy creeps me out, so I might be biased."

"If he creeps you out, I'll take your word that it's not smart to get involved. Women's intuition is worth listening to, I say." I looked at Noah.

"I'm not arguing. Thanks, Laura."

She nodded and headed back to the kitchen to check on our food. The diner was half-empty, so it was a good bet that nobody had paid much attention to our conversation. All the other patrons seemed engaged in their own conversations and meals.

"So, what do you think?" I leaned across the table. "We should check this place out, right?"

"For sure," Noah answered, "but we need to pray for protection before we ever walk through those doors. I don't want us walking unguarded into something like this."

"Good call. I'll give Josh and Lisa a call on my cell before we head over to Inner Pieces and ask them to be praying too."

Our conversation was interrupted as Laura returned with our meals. She was right; the cook did a great job with chicken and meatloaf. We were both so hungry that we hardly spoke until our plates were empty. Laura came back and cleared the table, leaving our bill. Noah grabbed it, and we headed for the till.

"Thanks for everything, Laura. Have a great night."

"You too – and take care."

Her expression was serious. I suspected she knew more about our intentions than we'd let on. I smiled reassuringly.

"We will."

The wind was cold, stealing my breath as we walked down the street toward the store we'd seen on our drive to the diner. It was only a block away. Noah took my hand and, even through our gloves, I could feel the heat of his skin. I loved that. I felt so safe when my hand was warm and tucked in his. A few feet from the storefront, he stopped, and we took a minute to pray together and then I called the Taylors to ask them to do the same. Reaching the store, he opened the door and let me walk through the opening ahead of him. The strong smell of incense clouded my senses as soon as I entered and I shook my head to clear it.

"Blessed be and welcome." As my eyes adjusted to the dimness inside, I saw a tall man walking toward us. "What in your life needs healing?"

I shot a nervous look at Noah, and his calm gaze reassured me.

"We just thought we'd look around, if you don't mind," he said.

"Everyone is in search of inner healing, even if they're not aware of it. The gods have directed your path here."

I edged back as the man stepped forward, his eyes dark with intensity.

"We serve our God, who does indeed direct our paths." Noah's voice was firm without being adversarial. "We're only here for information about the Children of the Elements. You were the high priest when they were in Lake Claire, weren't you?"

"I was. I have nothing to hide. What power does he have that compares to what I wield in this town? The authorities bow to me and believe everything I tell them."

"You seek power? I thought you said you were here to help people."

The man laughed, the harsh sound echoing in the darkened shop.

"I seek both. People come to me for help and give me power over their decisions, their habits and their lives. I force no one. They seek me freely."

"God will deal with your abuse of the innocent." Noah's eyes blazed.

"He may...if he exists. I'll take that chance."

I shivered and tugged at Noah's arm. "Let's ask our questions and get out of here. The darkness is more than physical. I'd rather not stay any longer than necessary."

Noah met my gaze and nodded.

"Who were the members of your cult in Lake Claire?"

"Why should I tell you?"

"Why shouldn't you?" I challenged. "If you're as powerful as you say, why shouldn't you tell us what we want to know? We want answers for two murders. If you weren't the killer, you have no reason to hide anything."

"Perhaps I have no wish to become involved."

I snorted. "I doubt that. Knowledge is power, right? Why don't you prove how powerful you are?"

He studied us, eyes shifting back and forth between my face and Noah's, before shrugging.

"It makes no difference to me. After all, my loyal," he smirked as he said the word, "followers in Lake Claire abandoned me when the Jackson family disappeared. Exposure after all this time is nothing less than their due. I'll write you a list."

He moved to the counter and pulled out a quill and piece of parchment. I shifted my eyes to Noah. Could the man be any more pretentious? Noah squeezed my hand in unspoken comfort.

"Here," Mitchell extended the sheet of parchment. "It's accurate to the best of my memory, and my memory is excellent."

Noah took it, meeting his gaze a final time. "Thank you." He paused. "You're wrong, you know."

"What do you mean?"

"Our God is not weak. His power is such that He could strike you dead with a word, but his strength is seen as much in His restraint as in His working. You should consider very carefully whom you have been serving. There will be no mercy for you if you do not bow your knee to him."

"Get out, and take your foolishness with you." He advanced toward us. "Get out, and never return, or you will face the true strength of my power."

"We'll leave, but you cannot touch us. Your power is nothing compared to that of our God."

Noah tugged me to the door, and we hurried through the opening. I breathed a sigh of relief even as the cold air struck my face, reddening my cheeks.

"Noah?" I tipped my face toward him, as we hurried down the street toward his car. "That might have been a very unwise thing for us to do."

"Maybe," his face was set like flint, "but I think it was necessary. We got the information we needed, and that man heard the truth. He's messing with forces he has no control over. They're using him. He's not using them."

"Perhaps," I said, shivering, "but his ears were obviously closed."

"That doesn't mean absolve us from the call to speak the truth."

"I never said it did." I agreed with him but that didn't mean I relished the encounter. "I'm just saying that I hope we don't end up in a situation like that again anytime soon."

"I hear you. Let's head home, Wynne, and drop by the Taylor's. I think we could use some people to pray and talk this over with."

"Now that," I replied fervently as he unlocked the car door and held it open for me, "is the best idea I've heard all day."

17

Large flakes of snow fell as we left Hastings and turned onto the highway toward Lake Claire. Noah tapped his fingers on the steering wheel in time to the music coming from the car stereo. I tucked my coat closer around me as I waited for the heater to kick in.

"I'm freezing," I said with a shiver. "Do you mind if I turn up the heat?"

"Go ahead. I'm not that cold, but you get chilled faster than I do."

"Thanks." I turned up the heater and then sat back, looking at the list lying on my lap. It was dark, so I could only make out its shape and not the writing on it. My curiosity was driving me crazy. We could wait until we were back in Lake Claire to look at the names, but I wanted to see them now.

"Will it bother you if I use light from my phone to read the names on the list? I'm not sure I can wait until we reach Lake Claire to find out who was, or is, involved in this mess."

Noah glanced over at me and smiled before returning his eyes to the road. "That's fine with me. I was hoping that your curiosity would be eating you alive so that I wouldn't have to ask you to read it. Saves face for me."

"Thanks a lot!" I lightly smacked his arm. "Way to make me feel like I have issues with impulse control."

"You're one of the unlikeliest candidates I've ever met for that particular problem, Wynne," he grinned. "You have your socks organized by color and style. That doesn't exactly shout lack of control."

"How do you know about that?" I was glad he couldn't see my red face in the darkened interior of the car.

"Sophie told me. She thought I'd find it cute, and I do."

"Huh. Well, as long as you think it's cute and not obsessive. I'm going to read the list. Do you want me to read it out loud?"

"That'd be great. I promise, I'll drive safe even if you're talking to me."

"I never doubted you would. Okay, here goes. The first name is John Simmons. Do you know him?"

"I've never heard of him. Next?"

"Tracy Card?" He shook his head. "Will Saunders? Sharon Smith?" None of the names sounded remotely familiar. I looked down and my breath caught in my throat. "Noah?"

"There's a Noah? Noah who?"

"No, I mean, Noah, you're not going to believe this."

"What? Who is it?"

I looked down again, studying the name. "It's Dan Black."

"Sheriff Dan Black? Are you sure?" he asked incredulously.

"It doesn't say 'sheriff', but I don't know of any other Dan Black in Lake Claire, do you?"

"No, but that would certainly explain a lot about the way the police handled things fifteen years ago."

We sat in silence for minute. We finally had a new lead, but how on earth were we going to pursue it? We couldn't exactly take it to the police, not with our new main suspect as the head of the force. I said just that.

"I know. There must be something we can do with this. Have you heard from Sophie if the feds are getting involved? Maybe we could pass it along to someone on that level?"

"She says not yet because neither of the bodies turned up to be missing persons in the federal database. That means that unless Sheriff Black requests federal assistance, it will remain a county investigation. Besides," I said as a thought struck, "we can't be totally sure that this list isn't an attempt to mislead us. I don't think the man we just left isn't exactly trustworthy."

"Good point. I think we should take it slow, but this list being inaccurate is a distinct possibility."

"I agree."

The lights of Lake Claire were visible as we passed the sign saying it was seven miles to town. Light filtered through the interior of the car from the headlights of a vehicle behind us. Noah was taking it easy with the speed, so we'd been passed a few times already. The light grew brighter as the vehicle drew closer, reflecting in the rear view mirror. Noah slowed a bit more and edged toward the side of the road to make it easier to be passed. I heard the sound of an engine gunning.

"I hate it when they do that, especially in winter," I said. "It always makes me nervous."

"It's probably a high school kid out for a joy ride with his dad's truck. He'll pass us soon enough."

The sound of the engine grew louder as the vehicle pulled up next to us. I could make out the outline of a truck, but it was too dark to tell what color or model it was. I could see the vague shape of a driver, but it was impossible to tell whether it was a man or woman. I swung my gaze back to the highway since watching the truck beside us was making me even more anxious. I was trying to relax by taking deep breaths when Noah hit the brakes.

"What the...?!"

"Noah? What's wrong?" Panic lanced through me. "What happened?"

"That truck just about veered right into us! I wonder if it's a drunk driver."

Noah slowed to a crawl, edging back into the right lane from the shoulder that we'd been forced onto. Thank you, God, that it's not icy yet!

"He's slowing down, too. Wynne," Noah's jaw was set. "Make sure your seatbelt is secure."

"I'm calling the police. Why would he be slowing down? That doesn't make sense? If he's drunk, he shouldn't even have noticed that we slowed down."

"I don't think he's drunk." The red light of the taillights ahead filtered over Noah's face, and I could see the tension on it. "I think whoever's driving that truck is messing with us on purpose."

I had my cell to my ear as it connected to county dispatch. I quickly explained our situation and location, agreeing to stay on the line.

"Noah, why would someone try to run us off the road? Do you think it's because of the list? If Mitchell didn't want us to have the information, he could have chosen not to give it to us, so it can't be him. But how would anyone else even know we have it?"

"I can't think of any other reason. The only people we told were Josh and Lisa. Someone in Hastings must have suspected what we were doing and followed us back to try to scare us off."

We were stuck behind the truck which was moving at a snail's pace. I looked at Noah, wondering what he was going to do. We could try to speed past the truck, or we could stop and hope that whoever got out didn't have a gun. Neither option seemed like a good one. Fear gripped my stomach with icy claws. *Jesus, please watch over us.* The faint sound of sirens reached my ears, and I let out a sigh of relief. We weren't out of trouble yet, but help was on the way.

"I'm going to pull over and wait for the police, okay?" Noah guided the car to the edge of the shoulder, slowing to a stop and putting it into park. He took my hand and held it as the taillights in front of us brightened when the driver of the truck also hit the brakes. For a minute, I thought the driver might pull over and approach us but the sirens were growing louder. The muffler roared as our assailant gunned the engine, whipping the truck off the highway and onto a side road a few feet ahead of us. The taillights vanished.

Looking down at my cell, I realized that, while it seemed endless, the whole encounter had taken less than ten minutes. I glanced up and saw a police car pulling to the side of the road and stopping in front of us. A figure emerged from the driver's side and headed toward us.

A tap sounded on the glass of the window. Noah rolled it down, and Sophie shone her flashlight in to illuminate the car interior. "Are you guys okay? What happened?"

"We're fine now, Sophie, thanks. The sound of the sirens scared the guy away," replied Noah, "but I'm pretty sure he had something up his sleeve. He tried to run us off the road first and then once he was in front of us, he kept slowing and trying to force us to stop."

Noah squeezed my hand before letting it go and gripping the wheel again.

"Did you get any details about the vehicle? Make or model? Color?" asked Sophie.

"Nothing but the basic shape of a truck," I said. "I couldn't even tell you if it was a man or woman driving. What about you, Noah?"

"I had my eyes fixed on the road. I didn't really see anything other than a dark truck."

"I'm going to ask you to come to the station with me anyway to take your statements, okay? The sheriff's off tonight, but I'll run this past him in the morning to see if he wants to follow up."

Noah and I exchanged a look. If the sheriff was off duty, it could have been him following us.

"We can do that. It won't take long, will it? Josh and Lisa are expecting us at their place."

"I'll make it as quick as possible," replied Sophie, "and then you can go. Follow me, and I'll escort you back to town."

She headed back to her patrol car and slid inside. We followed her lead all the way back to town, both of us quiet. As scary as was, what had just happened proved that we were on the right track.

"Maybe we should tell Sophie about the list, Noah," I said as we reached the town limits. "She might be able to help us get in touch with someone outside the county department who will investigate this further. I know we said we'd take it slowly but, I think after what just happened, we need to do something."

Noah remained silent.

"Noah? What do you think?" I prompted.

He sighed, rubbing a hand over his brow. "I don't know, Wynne. Maybe you should back off the investigation for awhile. Someone just tried to scare us off, and I have to say, they did a good job."

I sat back, stunned. "Are you planning to back off?" I asked softly.

"I have a responsibility to see this through. I made a commitment to print the truth in my paper. Someone needs to expose what happened. I'm just not sure it should be you, Wynne."

"I see. So, you'll continue to put yourself at risk but you won't allow me to do the same?"

"It's not the same thing. I'm trained to do this sort of work. It's what I signed up for when I started the paper. You don't have an obligation to the community the way I do."

"Trained? Since when does studying photography train you to investigate crimes? Don't you think I still have a responsibility before God to seek justice?"

"Yes, but he never said that you should try to hunt down a killer."

"He never said I shouldn't. I found those bodies. Maybe there's a reason for that. You said so yourself, don't you remember? I thought you understood how important this is to me."

"I know it's important to you. Why can't you see that your safety is important to me? I don't want someone finding your body next, Wynne. I couldn't bear that. Just step back. Please."

"How can you ask that of me when you're not planning to step back? Don't you think I worry about you?"

"It's not the same thing. I want to protect you."

"And I don't want to protect you? That's not a reason to stop looking for the truth."

"You're more vulnerable if someone tries to hurt you."

"Really. Because I'm a woman? I'm pretty sure that you being a man wouldn't make you impervious to a bullet. Come on, Noah. This is a ridiculous argument."

"Maybe it is, but why can't you just do what I'm asking you to?"

"Why can't you support me doing what I feel I need to do?"

"Wynne, someone is targeting you. First the doll hung on your door and now this? How am I supposed to stand by and allow you to continue putting yourself at risk? Just let me do it. I'll tell you everything I find out but you'll be safe."

I stared at his profile, his jaw clenched in determination. "I can't, Noah. I can't stop looking for the truth because it's dangerous and I hate that you're asking me to. It makes me feel like you think I'll get in your way or that I'm weak. I know someone is watching me, but do you honestly think they'll stop just because it appears I've given up? I don't think so. I have to trust God to protect me, as he has already. And, I have to trust Him to protect you too."

I fought back tears as Noah parked the car in a slot in front of the police department. How had things gone so wrong? We'd gone from excitement over a new lead to a yelling match in the space of an hour. We'd argued before but nothing like this. I opened my door and climbed out. Noah did the same and we walked silently into the station, the tension between us obvious. Sophie took one look at our faces and her eyes widened. To her credit, she didn't say anything about it. She led us to a conference room near the rear of the station and quickly took our statements. "Wynne? Do you have a minute? I want to ask you about your plans for tomorrow before you head home."

"I've got time. Noah, I'll call Josh and Lisa to tell them I'll be a bit late. I can walk from here to their place. You go ahead."

"Wynne, it's freezing out there. You said so yourself. I can wait for you."

"No, it'll be good for me. I need to think and cool off."

He studied me for a few seconds before nodding. "Okay. Listen," he lowered his voice as Sophie moved a discreet distance from us, "I'm sorry I yelled. I didn't mean to start an argument with you. I'm not angry at you, but I am angry that we even have to deal with this. I just want you safe."

"I know," I sighed. "I can't say I'm not mad either, but I'll get over it. I just don't know if I can do what you're asking."

"Fair enough, but I reserve the right to tell you what I think."

"Only if you're willing to hear what I think on the subject, and," I stressed the word, "try to see me as a partner in this. I get you needing to protect me, but statements that hint at my needing help are hard for me to swallow. It's a pride thing, and it's wrong, I know. I'm working on it."

"Okay. We're going to figure this out, Wynne. I promise."

"I *am* sorry, Noah. Forgive me for taking your words the wrong way and getting defensive?"

"You're forgiven. Am I?"

Relief coursed through me even though the fight had left me shaken. "Of course you are." I paused. "Are you still sure you want to be involved with me? We're probably going to have a few more fights on this subject alone. Is it worth it for you? Tell me now," I hurried on, "because if we keep on seeing each other and you decide you've had enough, it's going to tear me apart."

Noah's face softened and he cupped my cheek with his hand. "You're so worth it, Wynne. You make me angrier than anyone I know, but it's only because I," he stopped and cleared his throat before starting over. "It's only because I love you more than anyone I know, and I can't bear the thought of you being hurt. Or," his voice was quiet, "of losing you altogether. That would break my heart."

I felt tears spring to my eyes.

"You're sure?"

"I'm sure."

"Oh, Noah," I said, "I love you too. I have no idea how to handle this, but I don't want to lose you."

"You won't. I'm not going anywhere."

"Promise?"

"Promise."

He lowered his head and touched his lips to mine. I sighed and put my arms around his neck, moving into his embrace. The sound of Sophie's embarrassed cough registered dimly, but I didn't care. I was loved. It was enough. We'd deal with the rest later.

18

A week had passed since my argument with Noah. It still amazed me, I thought as I watched customers browsing the shelves in my store while rang books through the till, that he loved me. I'd yearned for that for so long, but had almost given up hope that I would ever meet someone I could love and trust. Now, in the space of a few short months, I had met and fallen in love with an honorable man who was so much more than I'd dreamt possible, and he loved me. A contented sigh escaped my lips as I scanned the bar code of the book in front of me.

"Thinking about something special?" Lisa asked, as she handed me cash to pay for her purchase, "Or should I say someone special?"

"Maybe I am," I smiled. "I promise, though, that my head is firmly set in reality when it comes to ringing your books through. I didn't scan any twice and double charge you."

"I believe you," she grinned back at me, "because I was

watching just to make sure. I saw your dreamy look the minute I walked in this morning."

I opened my mouth to argue, and then shrugged. She was right. I was daydreaming about Noah and the future often. The night before I'd almost clicked on a link to view engagement rings online and from there, I would have been wedding dress shopping. I didn't, but only because Sophie knocked on my door. After we'd had supper together and she'd left, I gave myself a strict lecture about waiting to look at rings–or anything wedding-related–until Noah brought the subject up. Unfortunately, that didn't stop me from checking out every set of rings I saw on my customer's hands to see what I liked best.

"What can I say? The man is just so distracting. He doesn't even have to try."

"I remember when I was dating Josh," said Lisa, leaning her elbows on the counter, "you couldn't get me to say two sentences without one beginning with 'Josh says'."

I laughed. "I'd forgotten about that. Remember when Julie Kingston asked what you thought of the pink dress she'd chosen for her first date with Dean Roberts and you said that Josh thought pink was evil?"

Lisa covered her face with her hands, moaning. "I wanted to die, I was so embarrassed. That was a good reality check for me, though. It was the first time I realized that not everyone needed to hear what Josh thought when they asked me what I thought."

"It was pretty funny, and it wasn't like Julie was offended. She was practically rolling on the floor, laughing, while you turned as red as a tomato."

"Tell me about it, and I will tell you this. A year of marriage will wipe that habit right out of you. I still value Josh's opinions, but

I no longer feel the need to spout them off to anyone who asks at the expense of my own. Sometimes I'm surprised he married me at all, since he loves it when I tell him what I think even when we disagree."

"I'm glad," I covered her hand with mine, "because those first few months you were dating were rough to watch. I was happy for you, but I was worried to see how much of yourself you were suppressing. I know part of that had to do with how young you guys were, but it was still hard to watch. I'm not doing that with Noah, am I?"

"No," Lisa's voice was firm, "you're not. Maybe if you'd met ten years ago, you would have, but not now. I hope you know that I'm just teasing you. It's wonderful to see how much Noah has softened you, even as your confidence has grown. He's good for you, Wynne, and from what I can see, you're good for him."

"Thanks. Your opinion matters to me. If you ever have concerns, Lisa, please tell me, okay? I know I'm probably not seeing as clearly as I need to, with my emotions so heavily involved, so I'm asking you and Josh to be straight with me."

"We will be, but I wouldn't worry about it. Josh says," she grinned widely, "that he thinks you and Noah are a great fit, and he's trying to keep his schedule clear for Saturdays about four to six months from now. You'll need someone to officiate the ceremony, you know."

"Stop!" I put my hands over my ears. "Thanks for the support, but I can't go there. I'm already fighting the urge to choose a ring and go dress shopping. I don't need any more encouragement."

Laughing, Lisa picked up her bag and headed toward the door. "You asked what I thought..." she let the sentence hang as she pushed the door open.

"I take it back!" I called my last remark out as the door swung shut behind her, cutting off the sound of her chuckling. I could see her shoulders still shaking with laughter as I watched her making her way down the street through the front window. I shook my head, smiling, and tidied up the counter. I'd given Jenny the day off, so the steady flow of customers kept me busy. Before I knew it, it was time to close the shop and go home to change before Sophie came by for a girl's movie night. Noah was busy trying to get the paper out for the following day and, besides, I'd hated getting ditched when my friends had started getting serious with a guy. I didn't want to do that to my girl friends.

I'd just fed Rochester and changed into a pair of comfy sweats and a t-shirt when there was a knock at the door.

"Hey Sophie," I said as I opened it, "come on in. Any idea what you want for supper? I have left-over chicken and rice or we could order something in."

"I'm not feeling picky today." She took off her coat and hung it over the back of a chair before crouching to pet Rochester. "Whatever you feel like eating is fine with me."

"Reheated chicken and rice it is," I replied, pulling the food from the fridge. "If we don't eat it tonight, I'll have to throw it out. I know," I turned around with a smile, "that's a shining endorsement."

Sophie shrugged and smiled briefly before wandering into the living room. Okay, I thought, something's up there. I ran through the past few days mentally, trying to think if I'd done something that could have offended her. Nothing came to mind. When Sophie and I disagreed, it was usually obvious, and we dealt with it right away. It wasn't like her to be so standoffish. I put the chicken and rice in the microwave and hit the reheat button.

"Sophie?" I asked, walking into the living room. "Is everything okay? You don't quite seem yourself tonight."

"I don't know."

"You don't know?" I moved closer, noting the shadows under her eyes. She was obviously having trouble sleeping. "What's going on?"

"Listen, Wynne, I need to tell you something. I should have told you a long time ago, but I didn't and now it's been so long and we're such good friends..." Her voice trailed off.

My stomach clenched as various scenarios rushed through my mind. Was she going to confess that she was in love with Noah too? That would be painful for both of us to work through. Or was there something about me that drove her crazy that she couldn't stand anymore?

"You can tell me anything, Sophie. You know that."

I sat down on the couch and waited. She dropped down to sit next to me, not meeting my gaze. "That's not my name."

"What?"

"I said that's not my name."

"Sophie's not your name?" I paused. "I've been calling you Sophie for months, and so has everyone else. I'm guessing we didn't all get it wrong when you introduced yourself."

"No, you didn't." She rubbed a hand over her face. "I lied, Wynne. Maybe not a total lie, but I haven't been completely honest with anyone."

"Okay. Why don't you tell me what you mean? I'm not going to judge you, Sophie."

"I know you won't. At least, I hope you won't."

"I won't. What is it, Sophie?" I stopped. "Wait, what do you want to me to call you?"

"You can still use Sophie," she said, her voice soft. "I had my name legally changed to Sophie Moore when I was sixteen. Before that," she paused and swallowed audibly, "my name was Amy." She lifted her eyes to meet mine. "My name was Amy Jackson."

I stared at her. The beeping of the microwave sounded faintly in the background, but I hardly noticed. For months, I'd been searching for answers. For months, she'd been saying she would help and for months she'd been hiding something that could change everything. Amy Jackson. She was Amy Jackson? Missing for fifteen years, Amy Jackson? I studied her face and saw, for the first time, similarities between her features and the image of fourteen year old Amy Jackson's face etched in my mind. I asked the first question that came to mind. "Where are your father and brother?"

"That's the problem, Wynne," she answered. "I don't know. That's why I came back to Lake Claire. I've been looking for answers of my own while you've been hunting for yours. I just," she stopped, dropping her gaze before forcing herself to meet mine, "I just couldn't keep this from you anymore. You're the best friend I've ever had and I don't want to lie to you."

I didn't know how I felt. Part of me was hurt. I had to own that. She hadn't trusted me with the truth. I could see not trusting me at the start, but it had been months. Still, I thought as I pushed that emotion aside, I couldn't blame her. She had a better reason than most for hiding, and it wasn't like I was the paragon of a trusting nature. She was telling me now. That was going to have to be good enough.

"I'm glad you're telling me now, Sophie. Amy," I corrected. "It doesn't matter that you didn't do it earlier."

"Please, call me Sophie. I can't tell anyone else, and I don't want you to slip up in public."

"Alright, Sophie. Listen, can you tell me what happened fifteen years ago?"

"I knew you were going to ask about that. I don't know," she held a hand up as I opened my mouth to ask another question, "I don't know. I was upstairs in my room, studying. Mom was in the kitchen, getting supper ready. Dad and Will were outside, I think. I'm not really sure. I know they were going to the garage to work on the car Will was trying to restore, and Mom was going to call us for supper." She cleared her throat, and I got up, fetching a glass of water from the kitchen. I handed it to her and she took a sip before continuing. "When Mom didn't call me by six o' clock, I closed my books and headed downstairs."

"What did you find?" I took her hand and squeezed it in silent support.

"Nobody was there. Supper was on the table but nobody was home. I called for Mom but no one answered. I checked the garage but Will and Dad weren't there either. I yelled outside, but it was completely quiet. I hadn't heard anything while I was upstairs, but I had music on and when I read, I tune out everything. I guess it wasn't surprising that I didn't hear anything."

"What happened next?"

"I went back into the house, and that's when I found the note."

"A note? From who?" Excitement rose in me, but I pushed it down. This was about Sophie's past, not my own questions.

"It was from Dad, and it was tucked under the little dish we used to store our keys. It said that he and Will were gone, and they wouldn't be contacting me again. He wrote that they'd come into the house from the garage around four-thirty to find my Mom," her dark eyes filled with tears, "lying on the kitchen floor, dead."

"What!? Why didn't they call the police?"

"He wrote that they couldn't because the police would think that he, Will, or even I had something to do with it. We were all involved with the Children of the Elements and the sheriff back then hated us. He figured that life on the run was no life for a teenage girl, but he could manage with Will. He said they "took care" of the body," tears were tracking down her cheeks steadily but her voice was clear, "but he didn't tell me what they'd done or where they'd gone. He just wrote that I should go to his stepsister's in Chicago, that he would make the arrangements for me to live with them. So," she finished, "that's what I did. I packed, hitched a ride from a trucker into a town about an hour from here and took the bus from there."

"Oh, Sophie," I slipped my arm around her shoulders, tears making their way down my own cheeks, "how horrible. Did you never tell anyone?"

"No. My step-aunt and uncle never asked. I don't know if anyone ever asked them about my family's disappearance but, if they did, my step-aunt and uncle would have had no qualms about lying to stay uninvolved. My dad always said his stepsister was a one of a kind woman, someone who could be trusted to keep a secret. I kept my head down, worked hard and entered the police academy right out of college. I always wanted to find out what really happened. but I didn't know how I was going to manage it. When the job opening in the sheriff's department here came up, I applied. I was trying to figure out how to ask around discreetly when you found the first body and blew that plan to pieces."

"Sorry about that. It was accidental, I promise."

She smiled weakly and dropped her head back against the couch.

"I know. The second one turning out to be my mom," she shook her head, eyes filling again, "threw me for a loop. I can't believe my dad just buried her under the porch, like trash! He loved her. I know he did, but we were all so screwed up."

"Most of us are," I murmured. "I sure am."

"Yeah, well you probably wouldn't hide a dead body."

"True. Good point." I gave her shoulders a squeeze and got up. "But they were afraid, Sophie. That accounts for a lot of the stupidity and selfishness in the world. What they did to you, and your mom, was wrong. I hope we can find them. Maybe more answers will help you forgive them."

"I don't want to forgive them. I just want to know what really happened."

I let that go. Now wasn't the time to talk about how bitterness could eat you alive. There would be the right moment for that another day. I put the food in the microwave for a couple of minutes again and then poked it with a fork.

"Sophie?"

"Yeah?"

"I know we need to talk about this more and make some plans, but I think we have a decision to make first."

She got up and walked into the kitchen, grabbing a tissue on the way. "What's that?"

"Chinese, Trudy's or pizza. What's it going to be?"

"I thought you reheated the chicken and rice." She looked over my shoulder at the dish sitting on the counter.

"I did. A bit too well, in fact, so unless you really like petrified food, we're going to have to order in."

The laugh that gurgled from her throat was weak, but it was there. That was worth wrecking dinner any day. I handed her the take-out menus from my fridge, and we sat down at the table to make the call. Since pizza was the easiest to eat in the living room, it got both our votes. I placed the order and we walked back into the living room to choose a movie.

"Sophie, are you okay with me telling Noah who you really are?"

She glanced over, eyes wary. "I'd rather you didn't, Wynne. The more people who know, the more likely it is that the secret will get out."

"Would that be so bad if it did? I mean, you've been hiding for years. You must be tired of living like this."

"I am, but I can't exactly go to my boss with this. At best, I'll get pulled off the case. At worst, I'll lose my job!"

"Okay, so we won't tell the sheriff, but I need to tell Noah. He can help, and he's proven he can be trusted, hasn't he? He hasn't told anyone that you're the source of a lot the information he prints, although people probably know since you and I are such good friends. It's logical. Besides, I can't keep something from him. It wouldn't be right."

"This town isn't exactly full of logicians, but I get it. Okay. You can tell Noah, but no one else. Do you promise me you won't tell anyone but him?"

"You have my word. We're going to find answers, Sophie. I know it. Things that hide in darkness are always exposed to the light, eventually. The Bible says that, and I've definitely seen God bring it about in lots of ways in my own life."

"Maybe, but I wouldn't count on God's involvement in this. He obviously wasn't around fifteen years ago when it all happened."

Her bitterness was clear, but I wasn't offended. It made sense, given what she'd been living with for the past two decades.

"He was there, Sophie. Just because He didn't stop it doesn't mean He didn't care."

"Whatever. Let's just pick something to watch, okay? I don't want to talk about this anymore."

"No problem. How about we watch something totally unrealistic and escape from everything for awhile?"

"A musical, then?" She raised a brow; her eyes tired but clear and meeting mine.

"Exactly. What do you feel like?"

"Wynne, they're pretty much all the same. Does it really matter?"

"Good point." I closed my eyes and picked one at random. "*Lucky Me*, it is."

"I hope that's a sign."

"Who knows?" I handed the DVD case to her as a knock sounded on the door announcing the arrival of our dinner. "I never know what God has planned, but I can tell you one thing. He's a God of justice. Even if it's not here on earth, whoever killed your mother will be called to account."

"What about that whole forgiveness thing?"

I glanced over my shoulder as I headed to answer the door.

"It's available for all who ask, but that doesn't mean that the truth won't be told. God is truth, He brings what is hidden in darkness into the light and exposes it. If the killer asks God, he or she will be fully forgiven, but that doesn't mean they won't be held responsible for making right what they can. True repentance involves owning our sin, admitting we can't make it right and then trusting God to do even while we accept the physical consequences."

"If that's what God is like, maybe. Not yet, but someday," she hurried on, holding up a hand to keep me from saying anything, "I might want to hear more."

"You name the day." I opened the door, paid for the pizza and brought it back into the living room, setting it on a tray so Rochester couldn't reach it. "Whenever you're ready, I'm here."

"Someday, then."

"Sounds good to me," I said, dropping slice of pizza on a plate and heading to the couch.

As the movie started, I took a minute to pray a blessing on my supper. *Would you keep softening her heart, Lord, and bring that "someday" around sooner than later?* I settled back to watch the movie when a thought had me bolting upright.

"What is it?" Sophie pressed the pause button. "Are you okay?"

"What about the arsenic, Sophie? Remember? Your mom's bones had evidence of arsenic poisoning."

"I don't know. That was the thing that pushed me over the edge to tell you. It's been haunting me ever since I found out, and I just couldn't bear it alone anymore."

Her expression was miserable, and I kicked myself for even bringing it up.

"Never mind. We can talk about it tomorrow. Maybe Noah will have something to add."

Sophie nodded and started the movie again. I settled back onto the couch, taking a bite of my pizza. My mind was whirling as Doris Day danced across the screen. With effort, I put the questions pouring through it away. Tomorrow, as I'd said to Sophie, would be soon enough to ask them. For now, I needed to be the friend she could count on to help her. Tonight, that meant relaxing.

"Maybe if we did our hair like that, guys would run their cars into stuff over us too."

"Wynne, I'm a cop," Sophie said dryly. "I'd have to ticket them and that would kill the romance before it started."

"Excellent point. It's probably not worth the effort. Or," I added, "the hairspray."

Snickering, she shoved my arm and then tucked her feet under her, settling into the couch. I did the same, determined to relax. Only God knew what tomorrow would bring, so there was no sense worrying about it now.

19

"Are you serious?" Noah's expression was etched with surprise. "She told you she's actually Amy Jackson?"

"Quiet," I hissed, taking his arm and hurrying him down the sidewalk. "She said I could only tell you. No one else. Obviously, we can't talk this out in public," I shot a meaningful glance at the crowd of people issuing from the doors of the church we'd just left, "but I didn't want to tell you we needed to talk without giving you the heads up. Otherwise, you might have thought we were headed for another argument, and that's just mean."

"I appreciate that," he smiled, "though, as a guy, my thought process would probably have been considerably less complicated. Odds are I would have thought if you said we needed to talk, that you wanted to talk."

"Sometimes I hate how uncomplicated you guys are," I grumbled. "It's not fair."

"Probably not," he said cheerfully, "but there's something really intriguing about the way you think. I like complicated."

"If you didn't," I nudged his arm, "we wouldn't be a good match, would we?"

"You said it. So, want to head to your place so you can give me the details or do you want to come over to mine?"

"Do you have food?"

"What a question." He sniffed disdainfully. "I always have food."

"Let me rephrase that. Do you have real people food for a grown up lunch?"

"Define 'real people food' and 'grown up lunch'. Do potato chips count? I think I might have some beef jerky too." I shot him a long-suffering look, and he threw up his hands. "What's that look for? I'm planning on grocery shopping this afternoon. And besides, beef jerky is practically its own food group."

"My place, it is," I said, taking his hand. "And while I'm fixing soup and sandwiches, you can tell me the latest news about the second body. Is it true that they've finally identified it?"

"That's what Sheriff Black told me himself," said Noah, as we climbed the stairs leading to my apartment.

I unlocked the door and let us in, crouching to pet Rochester as I walked past him into the kitchen to start lunch. I took of my coat and hung it on the back of a chair with my scarf and went to the sink to wash my hands. I pulled a can of Campbell's Tomato Soup out of the cupboard and held it up for approval.

"Works for me," said Noah as he slung his coat on top of mine. "Do you want me to start making some grilled cheese sandwiches?"

"You read my mind." I grinned at him, handing him the loaf of bread I'd just pulled from the freezer. "So, tell me all the details you got from Sheriff Black while we get this ready, and then I can tell you all about Sophie while we eat."

"It turns out," he said, placing a frying pan on the stove and turning on the element, "that the body in the clearing belonged to Mara Prentice, the former high priestess of the Children of the Elements. I only found out late last night. That's why I haven't told you this yet." He held up a hand to forestall my questions. "Sheriff Black actually called me around eleven. He said that he wanted me to put it in Monday's edition of the paper. He's hoping that maybe someone will come forward with information about when she was last seen so they can more accurately determine her time of death. All they know is that it was sometime in the past fifteen to twenty years."

"He has to know that it's connected to Mrs. Jackson's death," I stirred the soup on the stove and then moved out of the way as Noah dropped the sandwiches he'd made into the frying pan. "I know, I know," I said, rolling my eyes, "he needs concrete evidence, not suppositions."

"You can't blame him for that, since if and when they find the killer, they'll have to build a court case."

"I don't blame him. I just wish he would, one time at least, say what we're all thinking."

"I wouldn't hold my breath for that." Noah grinned. "He's been a cop too long to have normal human thought processes."

I laughed and picked up the soup pot, placing it on a pot holder I'd put on the table. Noah flipped the sandwiches onto a plate with the spatula he held, turned off the burner and followed me to the table. We sat, bowing to bless the food, and started eating.

"So, tell me more about Sophie's story. She just told you last night?"

"Right when we were getting supper ready," I confirmed, "which I then destroyed, so we had to order in. No comments," I gave him a warning looks as a grin flitted across his face, "about my cooking abilities. Anyway, she told me the whole story about how her family disappeared and she hasn't seen her father or brother for fifteen years. She has no idea where they are, but says that her dad left a note for her to find. It said that they had nothing to do with her mother's death, but they'd found the body and figured the cops would blame them so they ran. Her dad set up an arrangement for her to living with his stepsister and her family, so that's where she went. She hitchhiked part of the way, so that's why no one found a trace of her fifteen years ago."

"Does she believe that her dad is innocent?"

"I don't know," I thought for a minute. "I think so. She never said anything about him being guilty. She might not have wanted to go there though, even if she does want answers to her mother's death."

"So, how can we help her and how do we use what she told you to find out more?"

"That," I said, sighing, "is the problem. I have no idea how we're going to do this without tipping someone off. I promised her I wouldn't tell anyone but you, and even that was a stretch for her trust."

"I can understand that. Okay, how about this? Let's move forward as though we decided on our own to try to find the Jacksons. If the sheriff or anyone asks, we say we're looking for the family. We just don't tell them that we've already found the daughter."

"I don't know, Noah. Is that lying?"

"I don't think so. I think it's respecting Sophie's wishes while being honest about the fact that we're still hunting for answers. It's not going to surprise anyone that we're exploring new avenues to find the Jackson family."

I thought it over. "Can we just not say anything about the daughter at all? I'd be more comfortable if we do everything possible to remain totally truthful."

"Absolutely," he reached over and took my hand even though it was greasy from holding my sandwich. "I love that about you, Wynne."

"You love what about me, Noah?" I smiled at him, warmth spreading in my heart.

"I love your honesty. It's hard to say what I love most about you, but that's right up there."

"I love you, too, for so many reasons."

He leaned over and kissed me gently before pulling back. "I'd love to do some more of that," he rubbed a thumb over my lips, "but we did agree not to play with fire, right?"

"Right," I replied, feeling a mix of disappointment and caution. We were old enough to have a fair bit of restraint, but I definitely liked kissing him enough that we could get ourselves in trouble if we weren't careful.

"How about we clean up the dishes and take Rochester out for his daily constitutional?"

"Good idea. Not," I said with a wry look, "as tempting as your first one, but much wiser."

We quickly tidied the kitchen and put our coats back on. I grabbed Rochester's leash and jingled it. The sound had my lazy dog's head popping up, and he scrambled to his feet, rushing over to the door.

"Come on, boy," I said, rubbing his head as I attached the leash to his collar, "let's get you some exercise. You're getting pretty tubby. On you it's cute, but I think it makes me a bad pet owner."

"It does not," responded Noah, opening the door for me, "it makes you an easy mark, that's all."

"It's not just me, I'll have you know. He turns those big brown eyes on anyone, and they're putty in his paws. Don't think I didn't notice you slipping him beef jerky when you were over for a movie with Josh and Lisa a few nights ago."

Noah winced before shrugging his shoulders prosaically. "Busted. Rochester, this is your fault I'm in her bad graces."

"Blame the dog. That's mature," I laughed as we strolled down the sidewalk. He just smiled at me and squeezed my hand through my glove.

It was a mild winter so far, but it was still cold enough that gloves, scarves and a thick coat were a must. I breathed in deep, loving the smell of the crisp air even as it burned my lungs. Everything looked so pristine with a dusting of snow covering the grime of the previous year. Every season had its beauty, but winter held a special place in my heart. Most people see the absence of life in trees stripped of leaves and snow covering the grass, but I see barrenness that is necessary preparation for the new life of spring. There is a peace in the waiting that should be savored.

I was about to say that to Noah, when a car pulled up next to us. Glancing over, I saw that it was a police cruiser. Assuming Sophie was at the wheel; I waved and peered through the glass of the passenger window. To my surprise, I saw that the driver was Deputy Mason. Noah shot me a surprised look, eyebrows raised in question. I shook my head. As we stood watching, the deputy parked the car and climbed out, striding purposefully toward us.

"Good afternoon, folks," he said, touching the brim of his hat with his fingertips. "Out for a walk?"

"Is that a crime?" I could have cheerfully bit off my tongue as the question popped out of my mouth. "I mean, yes, we're enjoying our stroll."

"Good. Listen, the sheriff sent me to track you down. He wants to talk to both of you about the body we've identified as Mara Prentice. He said something about a connection between the victims."

We exchanged glances. If the sheriff wanted to talk, we should definitely listen. Anything he told us was bound to be useful. I looked down at Rochester. "Just let me drop Rochester off at my place, and we can walk over."

"He said to come right away, miss," Deputy Mason's voice was firm. "If you'll hop in, I'll drive you over myself. You can bring the dog. It shouldn't take long."

Given the way Deputy Mason had kept hitting on me back when I moved to town, I was hesitant to go anywhere with him. He'd toned it down some in the past few month, but he still made the odd attempt to flirt. At least I had Noah and Rochester with me. I nodded hesitantly, glancing at Noah to see what he thought.

"Sure. We can do that. Come on, Wynne, the sooner we go, the sooner we can get back to our day."

Deputy Mason opened the back door of the cruiser for us. I picked Rochester up and set him on the seat before climbing in behind him. Noah followed me in and the deputy shut the door before walking around to the drivers' side and getting in. He shifted it into gear and pulled away from the curb. I looked over my shoulder at the empty street we'd just been standing on before turning to face forward. The sheriff's department was two blocks down on the right. A thought struck me and I leaned forward, gripping the metal cage separating the front seats from the back with my fingers.

"How did you know where we were, Deputy Mason?"

"I tried your apartment first," he said easily, "and happened to spot you when I looked up and down the street. It was just luck, I guess."

"Right," uneasiness had my stomach tightening. "So the sheriff sent you to find us on a Sunday afternoon?"

"I just told you that." He glanced at me in the rearview mirror before returning his eyes to the road. "Why all the questions?"

"She just likes to know what's going on," replied Noah calmly. "It's a control thing. I think it's cute, but it drives some people nuts."

I whipped my head around to face him, hurt by the comment. He never talked about me like that. The warning I saw in his eyes stopped me short. His face was impassive, but his eyes were worried. I could see that, like me, he was having second thoughts about having climbed into the back of the patrol car. Stupid, I thought, we should have walked over ourselves. We should have checked in with the sheriff first. As if reading my thoughts, Noah reached over and squeezed my hand. Maybe it was nothing, but my uneasiness was growing even as we approached the station. The dread I felt was realized when, instead of pulling into the parking lot, Deputy Mason drove right past the station and continued on the road headed out of town.

"I thought you said the sheriff wanted to talk to us at the station," asked Noah casually. "You just passed it."

Deputy Mason said nothing as the car sped up. We left the town limits and he pushed the car to highway speed.

"Noah, what are we going to do?" I whispered, fear lacing my voice as I whispered the question.

"Stay calm, Wynne," he murmured, squeezing my hand. "I left my phone at your place. Do you have yours on you?"

I dropped a hand to my left pocket, nearly sighing with relief. The outline of the phone was solid beneath my fingers as I slid my hand over it.

"I've got it. I don't want to pull it out, though, or he'll see." My voice was barely audible even to me.

"Can you dial with it still in your pocket? I'll keep talking to him, and you call dispatch. Leave the line open, so we can tell them where we are when he finally stops the car. Deputy Mason," he raised his voice, "I demand you tell us where we're going. This is kidnapping."

I inched my gaze down. I could barely make out the keypad of the phone, illuminated while it still lay in my pocket. I sent up a prayer of thanks that it was still set to silent from the church service that morning. I carefully pressed the buttons, dialing the sheriff's department directly and praying that the operator would be able to hear us through the thick material of my coat.

"Deputy," I spoke loudly, joining Noah's barrage of questions, "Deputy Mason? Answer me. Why won't you tell us where you're taking us? Why did you lie about taking us to the sheriff's department? What do you want from us?"

He said nothing, eyes fixed on the road as the Jackson house loomed ahead to our right. The car slowed and he turned into the drive. For the first time in my life, I wasn't happy to see the isolated building. The very real worry that it might end up being my burial ground was making it hard to breathe. Please, Lord, let the phone be working. Let someone hear us. Send us help.

"Why are we here? You never said that you were going to take us to the Jackson house? Is the sheriff even meeting us here, or was that all a lie?" Noah carefully avoided my gaze as he tried to include as much information in his questions as possible. I hope whoever was listening on the other end of my phone–if someone were listening–was paying attention.

Without a word, Deputy Mason parked the car, turned off the engine and got out. He jerked open the back door, and I found myself staring down the barrel of his gun. "Get out."

I swung my legs stiffly out of the car and stood up, swaying a bit. I reached back into the car and lifted Rochester out, setting him on the ground. We moved to the side, as Noah climbed out slowly, eyes trained on Deputy Mason's gun.

"Into the house. Now."

"Okay. We're not going to try anything," said Noah, "so would you mind pointing that thing somewhere else?"

"Yes, I would. Get a move on."

Noah kept a hand on my lower back, guiding me forward as we walked toward the house. We climbed onto the porch, trying the knob of the front door when Deputy Mason gestured to it with his free hand. To my surprise, it opened easily. Walking through the opening, we entered the house. I'd wanted to do that for over fifteen years, but not at gunpoint.

I'd wanted answers too, but this wasn't how I thought I'd find them. *Lord, please, keep us safe. I don't want to die yet. I don't want to lose what Noah and I have before we even get the chance to make a life together. Give us more courage to say what needs to be said and do what needs to be done. Please, bring something good out of this horrible situation.*

20

I blinked, my eyes slowly adjusting to the darkness. The only light seeped in through dirty windows, leaving the impression that the room was more shadow than reality. I felt a tug on my hand as Rochester wandered further into the house, pulling at his leash.

"No, Rochester," I said automatically, yanking back. "Stay."

"Tie his leash to the newel post," Deputy Mason gestured toward the staircase leading to the second floor of the house, "and then come back here. Don't think I'm not watching you. It only takes a second to shoot someone. I should know."

"Listen, Deputy," Noah stepped cautiously forward, lifting his hands in surrender as the other man swung the gun back toward him, "why don't you just let us go? We don't even know why you've brought us here. Waving that thing," he gestured toward the gun, "around isn't going to help anything."

Deputy Mason laughed; the sound rusty and brittle. I kept my eyes fixed on Rochester, swiftly tying his leash handle to the post.

I tied it tightly. As much as I wanted to leave it loose so he could get away, I was worried that the deputy would shoot him if he tried to wander. Rochester growled low in his throat, hackles raised, clearly aware of my tension.

"It's okay, boy," I soothed in a whisper. "Just be good and sit here for awhile."

I stood up and walked back to where the two men stood facing off in the living room. In the dim light, I could see that it was still furnished with a couch and a couple of arm chairs. I wanted to drop down and give my shaky legs a rest, but I didn't want to give the deputy the satisfaction of knowing how scared I was.

"What do you want from us?" I asked, the steadiness of my voice surprising me.

"I don't want anything. It's too late for that. I have to fix this. Once you're both gone, and the questions will finally stop."

I met Noah's gaze, my insides turning to ice. Deputy Mason's eyes were over-bright, and his pupils were too dilated, even given the dimness of the room. If he wasn't on something, I thought, I'd eat Rochester's leash. I didn't know if Noah had noticed, but it didn't really matter if the man waving a gun at us was high or sober. He obviously intended to do us serious harm, regardless of what was coursing through his bloodstream.

"The questions won't stop, even if we're gone," Noah replied quietly. I wanted to kick him for saying it, but denying the fact was probably going to make the deputy even angrier than acknowledging it would. I hoped.

"They will! They have to! If you two weren't always stirring the sheriff up, he'd put this investigation on the back burner. Why should it matter? It's been fifteen years. Nobody missed those women then, and no one does now."

"Someone did," I eased my weight from one leg to the other, trying not to show the nerves running rampant in me. "What about the rest of Mrs. Jackson's family? What about Mitchell Lawrence, who was close to Mara Prentice when they led the Children of the Elements?"

"They weren't." Mason declared, eyes wilder than before. Spit flew from his mouth, and he dragged his sleeve across his face. "Mara wasn't with Mitchell. She wasn't."

"Okay," I said carefully. "She wasn't with him. I didn't know any better. I'm sorry."

His head jerked up and down. "That's right. You don't know. Nobody knows."

"What don't we know?" Noah's stance was relaxed, his tension only showing in the way he kept clenching and unclenching his hands. "You can tell us, Deputy. We're not leaving this house alive. It's clear you have no intention of letting that happen. What don't we know?"

As frightened as I was–and as desperately as I was praying for help–I was glad that Noah had named what we were facing. If we could convince Mason to talk and if we somehow managed to get out of here, there would finally be justice for Mara Prentice and Mrs. Jackson. If we didn't make it out alive–well, we both had something beautiful to look forward to after the brief pain of death. At least the pain would be brief.

"What don't we know?" I repeated Noah's words. "Tell us, Luke."

The deputy paced back and forth, muttering, gun still waving back and forth between Noah and me. He stopped after a minute, straightening his shoulders. "Okay. You're right," he nodded at

Noah, "I'm not letting you walk out of here alive. I'll get this off my chest and then–then it will die with you and I can be free."

We stood silent, waiting.

"It wasn't my fault," he began. "I never meant anyone to die. I was just a kid. I thought..." his voice trailed off, eyes staring off into the distance. He shook his head, recalling himself to the present. "She loved me, you see?"

"Who loved you?" I kept my voice gentle.

"Mara. She was so beautiful. I'd never seen a woman like her before. When we had our ceremonies, she singled me out, I could tell. I was fifteen when I joined the Children of the Elements, but she was something I never dreamt possible. She was everything to me."

His tone was reverent and his hand stroked the barrel of the gun, caressing it the way a lover would. "We used to meet in the grove, all of us. We celebrated the harvest and the new life of spring. Every season, we joined together and worshipped the elements–the earth. It was intoxicating; she was intoxicating. When she chose me, I was ecstatic. I'd loved her for so long, you see, and finally, she returned my feelings."

"How did she choose you?" I asked, sick at what I already knew was the answer.

"I was her partner in the ceremony that summer. Mitchell had told me that I wouldn't be allowed to participate until I was a man, but I knew I was already a man. Mara knew it too. She called to me one night, after a purifying ritual. She told me that she saw the light in me and, that together, we would be more powerful than I could imagine. She said to wait until everyone else had left the grove and then she would return. I did what she asked. After the grove was empty she came back, and we joined together for the first time to honor the gods and goddesses. It was to be a secret for the time being, she said, because Mitchell would be jealous of the power growing in me."

I could feel my face paling at the thought of the lonely fifteen year old boy seduced by the older, predatory woman. It was abhorrent. I saw by the look in Noah's eyes that he agreed, but he said nothing to indicate his feelings. Instead, he spoke softly and sympathetically. "No wonder you loved her. Sharing that act binds you in a way nothing else can, and you were young to experience such strong emotions. What happened then? How did it go wrong?"

"She lied to me," said Deputy Mason flatly. "She told me I was the only one she would be with, that together we would rule the Children. About a month after she and I came together, I was out walking near the grove, thinking of her. I heard something. It was her voice, but she wasn't alone. There was another voice with her. I hid in the trees and crept toward the clearing to see who it was. I saw Mitchell Lawrence there, lying with her on the grass. They had obviously just been together. In the ceremonies, she was with others, as the gods decreed she must, but she swore she would belong to me alone. We belonged to each other."

His face twisted with rage; the emotion still raw and powerful after fifteen years. I gripped Noah's hand, praying ceaselessly even as I listened.

"Mitchell left after a few minutes. Mara was lying on her back with her eyes closed. She loved," his voice broke, "to be one with nature. I knew that. I walked over and waited until she opened her eyes. I asked her how she could betray me this way, and she said..." His face convulsed, and his breath caught on a sob, "she said that it was fun while it lasted, but she was done with me. She wanted a real man again. She lied. The whole time we were together, it didn't mean anything to her."

"You must have been devastated," I murmured. My eyes caught the flicker of something outside the window, a large dark shape. I hurried to speak, hardly daring to hope that someone was there. "How could she treat you that way?"

"You see, it wasn't my fault. My hands were around her throat before I knew what was happening. If she hadn't lied, I wouldn't have done it! I loved her, I loved her so much," he repeated more calmly.

"Of course you loved her," Noah said, squeezing my hand gently as his gaze slid past the window. He saw it too, I thought, trying to breathe normally. "What I don't understand, though, is what happened to Mrs. Jackson?"

"That wasn't my fault, either," he spoke quickly. "She saw me and Mara in the clearing one time. She called me and told me she wanted to talk to me, so I came here." An angry flush darkened his cheeks, "She said that Mara was using me, that I had to tell Mitchell, so that he would cast Mara out of the Children of the Elements." He gave us a bewildered look. "Help him cast out the woman I loved? Why would I do that? But Mrs. Jackson wouldn't let it go. She said that Mitchell loved her, and that she was meant to be high priestess. She said that Mara was nothing but a cheat and a liar. When I refused, she said she was going to tell anyway, so I did what I had to."

"But Mara was already dead, wasn't she?" I asked, hoping the question wouldn't make him angrier. "Why did it matter what Mrs. Jackson was going to do?"

"She would have told everybody. It was our secret, and it was special. She would never have stopped trying to tarnish Mara's memory once she found out she was gone. Mara lied, but she didn't mean it. I know she didn't mean it. I had to stop Mrs. Jackson from telling anyone. I did what I had to." His voice lowered and sounded more natural, "It was worth it. It only took a few minutes. I held her throat and squeezed, and she was gone. I left the body and went back to hide Mara in the forest. I waited until nightfall, and then I buried Mara in the clearing, in our special place."

"Didn't you worry what would happen when someone found Mrs. Jackson's body?"

"I knew that the police would think it was her husband. I heard talk around town, and I even saw Mr. Jackson hit Mrs. Jackson across the face once during one of our ceremonies. When the family disappeared, I thought it would be over, and it was. It was over until you," he sneered, bringing the gun back to point straight at my face, "had to find Mara's body. Why couldn't you just leave it alone?"

Words stuck in my throat. It was clear that the time for conversation, for reasoning, was over. Sweat rolled down my temple, falling silently to the floor. Noah squeezed my hand reassuringly while keeping his eyes on Deputy Mason.

"The truth had to come out, Luke," he said. "It always does. It wasn't Wynne's fault that she stumbled across Mara's remains. You must see that. She didn't know the bones were there. Please, don't do this. Don't take another life, Luke."

The gun wavered but the deputy brought his other hand up to steady his aim. "I have to. I have to make you go away."

I saw his finger tense on the trigger and closed my eyes. *If this is it, I'm ready to see you, Jesus.* I was waiting for the sound of a gunshot when I heard something entirely different.

"Set the gun down, Luke. Set it down."

Sheriff Black walked softly into the living room from the kitchen. I didn't know how he'd done it, but he had managed to get into the house without any of us hearing him. I whispered a prayer of thanks and heard Noah doing the same thing.

"Sheriff, I can't. These two are dangerous. I've got them under control but the minute I take my gun off them, they're liable to try something. They'll tell you a pack of lies about the bodies Miss Forrester found. They're trying to pin the murders on me."

"Luke," the sheriff's voice was quiet. "I heard everything. I know. You need to put the gun down."

Deputy's Mason's eyes flicked wildly back and forth between us and the sheriff. He shook his head and wiped his nose with his sleeve, shifting his grip on the gun as he did. I flinched, praying it wouldn't go off.

"I won't. Sheriff, I won't go to jail. You know what they do to cops in there. I won't go."

"Luke, please, put the gun down."

"No," he yelled, his face contorted with fear. "I'd rather die than go to jail. You can't make me go." He swung the gun away from me and Noah, and I thought he was going to fire on the sheriff. Instead, he turned it toward his chin.

"No!"

The sheriff's cry and the sound of gunfire were simultaneous. I stood, stunned, as Deputy Mason dropped to the floor. A red stain spread from his shoulder, soaking into the fabric of his uniform shirt. His gun landed a few feet away from him, firing harmlessly into the wall as it hit the floor. I looked up, confused, as Noah slipped an arm around me. He nodded toward the front door.

Sophie stood in the entrance, arms still extended in proper shooting form. The smell of gunpowder hung in the air, drifting from the barrel of the weapon she'd just fired. Sheriff Black was on his knees next to Deputy Mason, his own uniform shirt off, folded and pressed down over the wounded shoulder to staunch the bleeding.

"Sophie, call for an ambulance. Quick."

"Yes, sir." She holstered her weapon and pulled out her radio. "Dispatch, we need an ambulance at the abandoned Jackson house just south of town. Officer down," her voice lowered, "I repeat, officer down."

The radio crackled to life. "Ambulance on its way, Officer Moore, do you need back-up?"

"No," she paused, eyes sad as she studied Deputy Mason's still form, "the suspect is in custody."

The radio crackled again as dispatch acknowledged her statement. She hung it back on her belt and walked over to where Noah and I were standing together, still in shock, hands held tight together.

"Are you alright?" she asked, her gaze running over each of us in turn. "Did he hurt you?"

"No, Sophie," Noah cleared his throat as his voice shook, "we're okay. Better than okay, now that you're here."

"I'm so glad to see you, Sophie," I let go of Noah's hand and threw my arms around her. "I thought this was it. I thought we were going to end up dead."

"You almost did," Sheriff Black spoke from his position near Deputy Mason's body. "A few minutes later, and we would have walked in on a bloodbath. You should thank your lucky stars that dispatch figured out your location from what you said and your phone's GPS, or you would have been dead."

"I think," I said firmly, "that I'll thank God for that."

"Me, too," Noah said. "If God hadn't been watching over us, Deputy Mason would have killed us long before you got here."

"Maybe," Sophie replied, "but I don't even want to think about it."

"Oh, Rochester!" I exclaimed, hurrying over to where he was lying near the stairs. He looked up at me with a mournful gaze. "I didn't forget you, I swear. I was just a little busy."

The dry look he gave me told me that my dog wasn't going to forget this slight anytime soon. I could probably look forward to chewed shoes for the foreseeable future. After what I'd just gone through, I didn't care. The sound of sirens grew louder as the ambulance drew nearer. I walked back to where Noah stood, pulling Rochester along with me.

"Can we go home now?" I asked. "It's been a really, really rough day."

"That might be the understatement of the year," said Sophie, a smile cracking her serious expression for the first time. "Unfortunately, we're going to have to take your statements before we can let you go. Sorry." She shrugged, shooting a glance at her boss.

"Take them back to the station and get their statements done with," replied Sheriff Black. "I'll be there soon to help you with that. I just want to get Luke on his way to the hospital and arrange a guard for him there. We'll have to keep him on suicide watch."

"Sheriff," I said quietly, "I know it probably doesn't help this feel any better, given that's your man wounded on the floor, but thank you."

"This wasn't your fault, Wynne," he looked up, "and neither was the whole situation. I know that. We'll talk more when I get to the station. Go on, Sophie, and head back to town."

With a nod, Sophie ushered us out the front door and into the sunny winter afternoon. My eyes were dazzled by the sudden light and I reached up the shade them. It felt like we'd been in the Jackson place forever but, I saw as I checked my watch, it had only been about twenty minutes. Twenty minutes, I thought with a shudder, in a house where I wasn't sure I would live or die. I felt Noah slip his arm around my waist, and I leaned into him. I was going to marry this man, I decided, and soon. Life was too short to second guess such a gift and I was never going to take it for granted again.

21

_____

The door to the small conference room opened and Sheriff Black walked in. Sophie looked up, reaching for the recorder she was using to take our statements. The sheriff nodded and she stopped it. I swung my gaze from her to the sheriff, noticing how tired and worn he looked.

"How's Deputy Mason?" Noah was genuinely concerned and his face showed it. "Sophie told us, when she came in after giving us a few minutes to get settled, that you had called to tell her they were taking him to surgery."

"Thanks for asking, though I can't see why you would care after what he put you through." Sheriff Black sat down and sighed heavily. "It looks like he's going to be okay. The bullet went clean through. Good shot," he flicked his gaze to Sophie, nodding at her, "and good timing."

"Thank you, sir. I was sorry I had to take it."

"You had to, Sophie. It was a justified shooting. You won't be under investigation long."

"I'm not worried, sir. If I hadn't taken the shot, Deputy Mason would have killed Wynne and Noah. As you said, a justified shooting."

"Yes, well," the sheriff cleared his throat, "are you about done taking their statements?"

"Yes, sir, we're just finishing up. Did you want me to start recording again?"

"Wait a minute. First, Sophie," he paused, looking distinctly uncomfortable, "there's something that I want to tell you before you turn that back on." He stopped, his gaze flickering over each of our faces before resting on Sophie's. "Do you remember me?"

"What do you mean, sir?" Sophie's tone was guarded. "I've been working for you for over a year. Of course I know you."

"That's not what I mean. Sophie..." he paused again. "Amy? Do you remember me?"

My mouth dropped open and I stared at Sophie. The shock on her face made it clear that she hadn't been lying when she told me I was the only person she'd revealed her identity to. I watched as emotions flitted across her face while she studied Sheriff Black closely–confusion, wariness and, finally, recognition.

"You were there." she cried. "I'd forgotten about you but you were there."

Noah leaned back in his chair, as entranced by the scene playing out as I was.

"Where was he?" I couldn't help blurting out the question even as Noah frowned at me. "At the ceremonies, is that what you mean? Well," I frowned back at Noah, "we know he would have been since his name was on the list Mitchell Lawrence gave us."

I slapped a hand over my mouth as Noah groaned. "What list is that?" Sheriff Black growled.

"That night that someone tried to run us off the road," I said sheepishly, "we were visiting Mitchell Lawrence in Hastings. We talked him into giving us a list of his followers from fifteen years ago, and you were on it."

"That's why we couldn't tell you about it," inserted Noah, trying to smooth over my untimely admission.

"That makes sense," Sophie said, "but why didn't you tell me?" Her eyes were hurt.

"I didn't want to put you in an awkward spot," I said, laying a hand on hers. "It wasn't because I didn't trust you, I promise. I was thinking about it when you told me you were Amy Jackson, and that revelation drove it clear out of my head."

She studied me silently before letting out a breath. "Okay. I get that. So, who else was on this list?"

"We can show it to you and the sheriff," I nodded at Sheriff Black, "once we're done here. Noah's got it at his place."

"Sheriff," Noah looked at the other man, "have you known that Sophie was actually Amy Jackson this whole time? Why didn't you say anything? And why didn't she recognize you, if you were both involved with the Children of the Elements?"

"I suspected before I knew," Sheriff Black said simply, "but I didn't say anything because I didn't want to tip her off. I thought that maybe she had something to do with the deaths of her mother and Mara Prentice. I'm sorry, Sophie," his eyes were regretful, "that I suspected you. It never crossed my mind that Luke could have anything to do with this. I knew that he'd been involved in the cult, but I watched him grow up after things fell apart. I was blinded by that, I think."

"I didn't recognize Sheriff Black because I wasn't actually a member," interjected Sophie. "I stayed on the fringes and never participated in the ceremonies, only in the public meetings. My parents never allowed me and my brother to join them in the ceremonies, thankfully, but Will snuck out and watched what went on there a few times. He never said anything about you being there, Dan."

"I was looking for something–for answers to why I was even on this earth–but I wasn't ready to commit." Anger darkened the sheriff's cheeks. "When I realized that all the talk about harmony and union with the earth actually meant orgies and unquestioning obedience to two people calling themselves priest and priestess, I left. I was working for the department as a deputy already, and I knew what they were doing was skirting the line of legality. Even with everything I saw, I never suspected that Mara Prentice was the kind of predator that would seduce a teenage boy."

"Why not?" asked Sophie, her voice bitter. "Mitchell Lawrence sure didn't have a problem trying the same thing. He tried to talk my parents into offering me up as a 'gift to the goddess of the earth' the year my mom died. Dad said no way, but Mom was infatuated with Mitchell and pushed for Dad's agreement. She even tried to convince me to go of my own free will. She said I still wouldn't be allowed to be part of the ceremonies, but I would be a special offering."

Something clicked in my mind as she spoke. "Is that," I asked quietly, "why you decided to poison her with arsenic? Because she was going to force you to give yourself to Mitchell Lawrence?"

Understanding also dawned on Noah's face. "That was it, wasn't it? We were trying to figure out why someone would poison her over time and then just kill her outright. It wasn't one person, was it? The poisoner was you."

"Sophie?" Sheriff Black spoke softly. "No one is going to judge you for that. You were between a rock and a hard place–and you were a child."

"It wasn't me, Sheriff," she answered firmly, lifting her chin. "I know you expect me to deny it. I don't know that I would admit it if I had been poisoning my mother, but it wasn't me."

"If it wasn't you, who was it?" asked Noah. "If the motive was your safety..." his voice trailed off as a thought struck, the same, I was sure, that struck me.

"It was your brother, wasn't it?" I asked. "I thought maybe your dad, but he was so deeply entrenched in the Children of the Elements, he wouldn't have resisted their plans. But your brother? He would have wanted to protect and he had no way to get either of you away from your parents."

Sophie stared at her hands, fingers tightly clenched.

"Sophie?" Sheriff Black prompted.

"I don't know, Sheriff!" Sophie's face twisted with grief. "I've never known for sure. If I had to guess," she spoke more slowly, visibly trying to calm herself, "I would say my brother was far more likely to try to help me than my dad. I saw him once, washing coffee grounds off his fingers in the kitchen sink. It didn't make sense, since he never touched the stuff .We were only teens."

"Wouldn't that have affected your dad too?" I asked. "If your brother put the arsenic in the coffee grounds, anyone who drank the stuff would get the poison in their system."

"Dad never drank coffee," replied Sophie. "Mom loved it, though. She had to have at least two cups a day, sometimes more than that. Listen, Sheriff," she turned to her boss, "I'm still trying to find my dad and brother. I can't do that, in good conscience, if I know my finding them is going to mean that my brother will be prosecuted for something he did to try to save me."

"The matter is closed, as far as I'm concerned," responded the sheriff, meeting her gaze squarely. "There's no proof your brother did anything other than make coffee and get grounds on his fingers–and we only have your statement for that. Your mother was killed by Deputy Mason. We have his confession. Nobody should question anything further, but if they do, I'll deal with them. If you find your brother, all he'll get from me is a handshake and my thanks that he tried so hard to keep you safe."

Sophie blew out a long breath. "Thank you." Her voice trembled. "I don't know what I would have done if you decided to go after him. I love this job and this town."

"As far as I'm concerned," said the sheriff, "you're not going anywhere. I'm going to need you to work even harder now that I'm down a deputy."

"Consider it done."

"There's just one more thing," he faced Noah and I once more. "I need to ask you to forgive me. If I had been honest about my history with the cult, maybe it would have been harder for Deputy Mason to hide his past. If I'd talked about my involvement, his very likely would have come to light."

"His actions aren't your fault, sir," I said as Noah nodded. "Deputy Mason made his choices."

"I know," he responded, "but I also made mine, and they were wrong."

"Then you're forgiven," Noah said. "The matter is done. You have our trust," he glanced at me as I murmured my agreement, "and our support as you move forward with building your case.

We've been compiling information for months, and you're welcome to everything we have, right, Wynne?"

"Absolutely. I'm quite ready to be done with murder for the foreseeable future."

"Sophie?" Sheriff Black sounded unnaturally tentative. "What about you?"

"There's nothing to forgive, Sheriff," she replied evenly. "I've made my own poor decisions lately. Whatever absolution you want is yours."

"Thank you. Now," he straightened, shoulder squaring and voice firm, "let's get the rest of your statements on record, so you can get out of here."

"That sounds perfect." I squeezed Noah's hand. "There's a lot that I have to say to this man, and I'd prefer not to do it in public."

"That sounds equal parts ominous and intriguing." Noah laughed as he squeezed my hand in return. "But since I have a lot to say to you as well, it should be an interesting afternoon."

"I hate to break it to you," said Sophie dryly, "but it's probably not going to be as interesting as the last few hours were. There's not much that's going to top being held at gunpoint."

"I don't know about that," Noah smiled enigmatically. "I might have something up my sleeve that will beat it."

My heart fluttered at what I hoped he was saying. Not getting shot already made this a landmark day. If I ended it with something shiny on the third finger of my left hand, I just might faint.

The grin that spread across Sophie's face said that she was thinking the same thing I was. "Let's get this done, then," she said, giving me an obvious wink, "and you two can head home to have your talk.

She touched the button to start recording again. "This is Officer Sophie Moore with Sheriff Dan Black, continuing interview with Wynne Forrester and Noah Sutton regarding their abduction by former Deputy Luke Mason. Miss Forrester, Mr. Sutton, if you could describe the situation for us one more time, how did Luke Mason convince you to enter his vehicle?"

As Noah began to recount the story once more, I allowed my thoughts to drift. When I had moved to Lake Claire almost a year before, I had come with the hope that I would find a place to belong. I had hoped that this place would become my home. My prayer had been for that one thing. God, in the same way he so often did, had completely surpassed my expectations. Where I had asked for a place to belong, he had given me that along with someone to belong to. Where I had asked for a home, he had given me a community. Shame on me, I thought, for acting as though he was not capable of more than I could ask or imagine.

I'm so thankful, Lord. I don't say it often enough but I am. I'm thankful for this life, for the fact that you saved it two thousand years ago in what you did on the cross, and that you saved it two hours ago by sending Sheriff Black and Sophie in time to help us. I'm giving you my future. It looks like that's going to include Noah, so I'm giving you him as well, and am asking that you guide us clearly to what you want. And if I freak out along the way, as you and I both know I probably will, I'm praying that you won't let me run from what you have planned because your plan is best. That's what I want.

"Anything you want to add to Mr. Sutton's statement?" Sheriff Black's voice cut through my prayer.

"No, sir," I said with a slow smile. "I think I've said everything I need to."

22

The news of Deputy Mason's arrest was all the town could talk about in the weeks that followed. The case never made it to trial. Luke Mason took a plea deal from prosecutor's office, confessing that he killed both Mrs. Jackson and Mara Prentice in exchange for a lesser sentence. He also confessed to leaving the death threat on my door months before he attempted to kill me and Noah to stop our investigation. He was currently serving two consecutive life sentences with no chance of parole, along with five years for attempted murder in mine and Noah's case. The prosecutor dropped the charges on the death threat, and I didn't mind. Luke Mason would spend the rest of his life behind bars.

Noah and I went to visit him once after he'd been sentenced. I admit, I was hoping that he would apologize or ask our forgiveness, but that didn't happen. In his mind, he was justified in what he tried to do. We were a threat to his way of life, and that made us expendable. We offered our forgiveness anyway. I was glad we did, because three weeks later, he was stabbed with a homemade shiv in the prison showers by another inmate and bled out in minutes. The very thing he'd been so terrified of actually happened. I only hoped that he'd made peace with God before he died. It didn't seem likely, but I had to leave his soul in God's hands.

Dan Black stayed on as sheriff. If he'd had doubts that the townspeople would trust him after his involvement in the Children of the Elements came out, they were quickly alleviated. If anything, people opened their hearts to him when they saw how much he regretted his silence and the issues it caused. Sophie had been promoted to deputy and there was a new officer on staff as well. This one had no ties to the town, so the likelihood that the sheriff's department was harboring another former member of the local cult was pretty low.

Once his past came to light, Sheriff Black went right to work cleaning up the town. After tying up loose ends with the Children of the Elements investigation, he ended up exposing a group of men within the town leadership that were embezzling from the town's funds. That trial begins next January, and Noah's been covering the investigation from the start. His paper is doing really well. The fact that the *Lake Claire Gazette* folded when his uncle was arrested as part of the embezzling crew didn't hurt his circulation, that's for sure. Noah, with a show of character that I was so proud of, was meeting with his aunt and cousins once a month to try to re-establish relationship there. He offered to do the same with his uncle, but Ellis Porter said he'd rather eat glass than spend one minute with the nephew who "entrapped" him and his cronies by making up the embezzlement story. His loss, I say, and Noah seems to be okay about it. We're both learning a lot about extending grace.

That seems to be working out well for us in our marriage, too. We got married in the spring, much to my grandparent's delight. I thought they were going to faint from relief when I told them I was engaged. Our relationship is more relaxed for me now that I'm safely attached to a man.

The store's been doing well. It's busy, but I like that. We have a little extra income now that I'm renting the apartment to Sophie. She wanted something a little nicer than her basement suite but not quite as permanent as a house. She's not quite ready to set down roots yet. I think once she finds her dad and brother, she might be able to make that commitment. She has made one really important commitment, though. After the whole incident with Deputy Mason, especially his death in prison, she started asking me a lot more questions about God. Those conversations led to her getting to know Jesus in a personal way.

She was also spending time with Mr. Patterson and Father Bryce out at the Piney Ridge senior's complex. She told me a few months ago that she felt like she'd found two fathers to take the place of the one she'd lost. I hope that, even if she never does find her dad and brother, she'll consider those two, along with me and Noah, her family. I think she already does. We have her over for supper at least once a week, and she and I still have regular girl's nights. Noah usually spends those with Mr. Patterson and Father Bryce. What they do for guys' night, I don't ask–though Noah always comes home laughing over their latest antics.

As busy as we are, I wouldn't change my life for anything. When I reach down to put a hand on my growing belly, I'm awed at this evidence of the new life that's due to arrive in less than three months. Noah and I are alternately terrified and thrilled that we're expecting not one, but two little ones. Doubly blessed, that's what Noah said. I agree when I don't feel like slugging him for his part in making me as big as a house. We're both prepared for the fact that he'll likely get hit a few times during labor. He says he doesn't care. I told him I'd hold him to that.

I may feel as big as a house but I'm nowhere near the size of the house we bought and renovated.

The abandoned Jackson home was abandoned no longer. As a wedding present, Sophie had gotten in touch with her step-aunt and convinced her to sell the place to us. The renovations had taken a lot of time, and more money than we'd planned on, but the result was the stuff of dreams. All traces of the tragic lives of its former inhabitants were gone, as were those of Deputy Mason's attack. Noah and I decided soon after the abduction that we still loved the house, despite what we'd gone through. It seemed fitting that we do something to redeem it, to bring it back to what it was meant to be. Every day, when I wake up to sunlight slanting through the windows and the breeze drifting in through open windows, I'm reminded of how far God has brought me. The memory of what began fifteen years earlier as heartbreak and misfortune simply emphasizes his ability to restore anything. He took a place that once housed death and made it a sanctuary for the new life that Noah and I were living.

I looked out the window and saw the cloud of dust that heralded Noah's arrival home from work. I walked over to the front door, opening it and stepping out onto the porch as he climbed out of the car. He looked up and smiled, gaze dropping as it always did these days, to my stomach. He locked the car and climbed the steps, reaching out to take my hand. I lifted my face for his kiss. His lips touched mine gently, then a bit more firmly as he rested his free hand on my belly.

"Welcome home," I said after I caught my breath. "Supper's just about ready."

"It's good to be home," his smile widened. "Come on, tell me all about your day while I get supper ready. You can sit down and relax."

"I thought I was cooking today. I've already got a roast in the oven. It's just the potatoes and veggies that need fixing."

He looked at my stomach again. "You're cooking all day, every day, Wynne. Let me handle supper tonight."

I laughed and tugged him into the house. As the door swung shut behind us, I offered up a prayer of thanksgiving. The past was gone, the present was breathtaking and the future was bright. I reveled in the feel of Noah's hand in mine, in the firmness of the glowing hardwood floor under my swollen feet and the savory smell of the roast in the oven. Leaning my head against his shoulder, I sighed in contentment. *You have given me more than I ever dreamed possible, and I don't have words enough to say how I feel. Just thank you.*

I breathed deep, inhaling the lingering scent of the soap my husband had used that morning. *Just thank you, Lord. Thank you.*

CPSIA information can be obtained at www.ICGtesting.com
Printed in the USA
LVOW09s0700290315

432425LV00010B/139/P